LOVE WASN'T BUILT IN A DAY

DESIRING THE DEXINGTONS
BOOK ONE

RENÉE DAHLIA

FOREWORD

Welcome to *Love Wasn't Built In A Day*, the first book in the Desiring the Dexingtons series. This is a Regency romance series based around Humphrey Dexington and his seven sisters. The Dexington family own a linen mill and do various things with business and fabric...

If you love friends to lovers, then you'll enjoy *Love Wasn't Built In A Day*.

Please note that because this book is set in the Regency period, it includes discussions around sodomite laws, and slavery.

This book is written in Australian English and some spelling and phrases may be unfamiliar to American readers.

If you are keen to keep up to date on new releases and, more importantly, sales, I recommend you sign up to my newsletter at www.reneedahlia.com.

I hope you enjoy reading this book!

Renée

ABOUT THE AUTHOR

An avid reader, Renée Dahlia writes contemporary and historical queer romance. Renée is a bisexual cis-woman who is fascinated by people and loves to explore human relationships, with a side of humour, through her writing. Renée has a degree in physics and mathematics, using this to write data-based magazine articles for the horse racing industry. Her love of horses often shines through in her fiction, and she loves a good intrigue and to escape the real world in the pages of a book. When she isn't reading or writing, Renée spends her time with her four children, usually watching them play cricket.

You can read more about Renée's author journey on her about page at www.reneedahlia.com

LOVE WASN'T BUILT IN A DAY

A friends to lovers gay Regency romance with a delicious slow burn.

HUMPREY DEXINGTON wants his best friend, and colleague, to be happy in love. With him, preferably. After accidentally reading a letter written by David to a former lover, Humphrey realises his own love for David would forever remain unrequited. It's time to finally move on and let David find someone to love who would stick by him. If he couldn't have David, at least David could have the man who he sent such poignant letters to.

Humphrey invites David and his lover to the Soho Club for an evening together, but when David's lover doesn't show, it might just give Humphrey the chance he's always wanted.

Engineer DAVID MATTSON doesn't have time for love. Grand engineering projects dominate his life, and he spends most of the year travelling to supervise the works. When his last affair ended, he decided that was it. Love wasn't for him. He'd never find someone who wanted to share the life he adored, who would travel with him, and care as deeply for every detail of every bridge and drain and lock.

Slowly, David realises that person has been beside him, loyal to him and his beloved engineering, for the past decade. All he needs is to be brave enough to say yes to Humphrey's love.

CHAPTER ONE

"The Prime Minister has been assassinated." One of the Mrs Skarsgards burst into the Soho Club with such dramatic overblown news that Humphrey glanced sardonically at David. The news couldn't possibly be true; Prime Ministers didn't get assassinated in England. What a load of rot.

"I told you this was the place to be." Humphrey let sarcasm fill his voice as he leaned back against the dark velvet covered chair and crossed one leg over his knee. "A place where wild rumour abounds, where people like us can be free with our affections without fear, and a place where people can have a solid—" Humphrey paused—solid, not sordid—holding back on more erotic thoughts inspired by the wonderful establishment that was the Soho Club. "—intellectual discussion."

David looked askance at him. "I have several intellectual

discussions every day in the course of my work." David leaned forward a fraction, his hand wrapped around a glass of whisky.

"Why thank you. I take that as a compliment." If he'd been standing, Humphrey would've bowed, if only to get a reaction from David. They'd worked together for a decade, with Humphrey gradually falling deeply in love with the focused engineer in the process. They made an excellent business partnership; Humphrey overseeing the funds, both acquiring money from governments and investors, and ensuring that every project stayed on budget. And David. Well, David would go down in history as one of the greatest engineers of all time.

Humphrey wanted two things—David in his arms, and more importantly, for David to truly see him as someone valuable to him. Loyal and clever. The best at what he did.

"Do you think the news is true?" Doubt infused David's voice and Humphrey twisted to stare at him.

"I suppose there is an outside chance. Do you think it could be the Luddites?" His sisters, particularly Elspeth, were concerned with the recent uprisings and how they might affect his family's linen manufacturing business.

David frowned. "There are many reasons why someone might go to such drastic measures."

"Do you harbour a secret desire to assassinate someone?" As soon as he spoke, he regretted it because the look of disdain David sent him was enough to cut him. This—his lackadaisical charm—was why David would never take him seriously as a potential lover. For years, Humphrey had watched David have affairs with other men, knowing that

David didn't see him like that. The pining was completely one sided and Humphrey hated that he'd never be enough for David. He knew this because none of the other brilliant men had lived up to David's lofty standards. Each of David's affairs were with someone utterly outstanding in their chosen trade; the very best stone masons, poets, military leaders, and musicians. The pattern of David's preferences for men who stood above others should have been intimidating. Humphrey shook off the doubt—no other business person could have spent ten years at David's side keeping his ambition and achievements on track. He knew he was the best at what he did. He only needed David to see it.

The silence stretched out and every second seemed like David disrespected him more and more.

David finally cleared his throat. "We have been business partners for a long time now."

Ten years and two months, to be precise, which didn't answer the question as to why David would mention it. "Yes."

"Then I know I can trust you with this. There is a man who I've come to despise."

Humphrey pinched his lips together, so he didn't blurt something he'd regret. He nodded as solemnly as he could manage, and hoped he looked encouraging and supportive.

"Lord Hansberry."

"I understand the sentiment. The way he's blocked further funds on the Caledonian project is highly frustrating." And Humphrey knew it was personal. Lord Hansberry was married to Humphrey's mother's cousin; and the family lore was that he carried a grudge against Humphrey's maternal grandfather, Lord Langston. Humphrey's involvement with David's work was a direct link to some of David's biggest financial problems.

"Yes. I've often wondered how much more progress we could make if he were out of the way."

"On that, we agree most whole-heartedly."

David closed his eyes for a moment, and when he opened them again, the fierce sparkle had faded. "I could never do it. It is one thing to want to demolish an obstacle in one's path, much like a pesky hill, and completely another to wish the demise of a human by one's own hand."

"No one would dare accuse you of such a thing, David." A more ethical man couldn't be found in all of England. David was driven to create canals and roads because they benefited the people who lived near them. Good transport created trade opportunities and allowed people to improve their lives. When their projects went over time or over budget, it was always because David cared for people eking out a living in the toughest conditions. His determination to finish projects under the worst circumstances came from David's own experiences. David had grown up with nothing. He understood the struggle for a better life more than anyone else Humphrey knew.

The job of building large scale projects was a dangerous one that required people with incredible toughness and stamina, and while David pushed people to work hard, it was much better for the project to keep everyone alive and healthy than to waste time and money on continually finding replacements. When outlined like that, it sounded slightly callous, except David cared; for his workers, and for the people who would benefit from the completed project. It had to get done.

"I will find a way to get the necessary funds." Humphrey doubled his determination. He would have to speak to a few old school friends, a few words in the right ears, to get the next rounding of funding passed.

"A lack of Prime Minister might be an opportunity."

"Yes. When or if the unlikely news is confirmed, I will get to work. Until then, we should enjoy the delights of the Soho Club." Humphrey glanced at the small string quartet in the corner of the room which entertained the few guests. The bright cheery tune they played had the elements of the waltz, a scandalous dance, and exactly the style of music one might expect from a club such as the Soho where people came to be free from the bounds of society's rules. It wouldn't surprise Humphrey in the slightest if they next played a Spanish bolero since the new-fangled dance was causing the strait-laced members of the ton to need burned feathers. As usual, the quartet stood in the corner of the room near a fireplace. A much needed heat source, given they wore no clothes. The man holding the double bass had the most spectacular chest and forearms. His instrument hid much of his body; a tease.

"I find myself too down in the dumps to enjoy myself." David confirmed what Humphrey had suspected for a few weeks. His latest affair, with the poet Mr Sutherland, had ended and David hadn't recovered as fast as usual. Humphrey suspected that David had fallen in love with the poet, a notion that formed a bitter lump in his chest. Yesterday, when looking for an invoice among David's papers, Humphrey had read a half-drafted letter in David's hand.

"A man more heartily to be liked, more worthy to be esteemed and admired I have never fallen in with; and there-

fore it is painful to think how little likely it is that I shall ever see Sutherland again."

Humphrey realised he would always be an inadequate substitute for David's missed love and he'd resolved to give up his yearning for the incredibly energetic engineer. If he couldn't have David's love, he could be a good friend, hence why they were seated in the Soho Club together. There was no better place to push Sutherland and David together, in this place where all manner of delights were on offer and rooms for privacy were readily available. And if it didn't work out with Sutherland, at the very least it might help David if he used the Soho Club's facilities to bury his broken heart in a comforting body. Preferably his. He cleared away the roughness in his throat caused by that stray thought. That was as unlikely as the Pope visiting this establishment. His heart skipped a beat. His plan to stop loving David wasn't going very well at all.

CHAPTER TWO

David knew the news had to be true. Damn. The Honourable Spencer Perceval was a devout Christian who had all the faults that came with those beliefs. David took care with his speech and actions around people like Perceval because their narrow views weren't very accepting of men like himself who loved other men, and they would never hesitate to enforce the law against him. His achievements, and the good he created for many people, mattered for naught against the weight of the church and the law. If they knew about his choice of lovers, he'd be dead. Simple. The news of Perceval's demise shouldn't cut him like this, except it did. For one good reason.

Perceval believed in his engineering projects.

David had lost an important political ally, and right at the point when the Caledonian Canal project was an utter disaster. It would take a miracle, like Lord Hansberry changing his mind on allowing access to his land, to pull success out of this current mess. The terrain was tougher than he'd expected and the weather in the Scottish Highlands made working in winter impossible. He'd planned everything based on the highly successful Welsh canals and it had been a mistake to assume a similar timeline given the challenging terrain and weather in Scotland compared to Wales. The project dragged on and on and he was under more pressure every year to show progress. The challenge created by Perceval's unfortunate demise would have to inspire him to work harder. It was exactly what he needed after Sutherland's rejection. A jolt to bring his focus back to his work.

"I'm surprised someone would assassinate Perceval. He was an oddly quiet character but he had many allies." Humphrey, once again, had a flippant comment. David ground his teeth together; his business partner had a knack for prodding him in just the wrong way.

"And enemies. He was one of the champions of the Abolition of the Slave Trade Act, and when that quite rightly passed, it cut into the incomes of many of the richest families in the land." David had tucked away the information on who stood against the necessary law so he would never work with them. Perceval might have wanted to see David hang for his desires, but he was completely right on the abhorrent matter of slavery. The law had passed only five years ago, and still people fought for their rights to own other people. David found the concept repulsive and sided with those who wanted broader reaching laws; it wasn't enough to stop transporting people into slavery. The entire sick notion had to be stopped. "And do you recall, Perceval had been the lawyer who'd defended Princess Caroline. A rather divisive case. Of course the Luddites hate him too as he protected industry and manufacturing."

"Once again your memory is excellent. Are you an ally or an enemy?" Humphrey glanced at the front door.

David tried not to growl and instead leaned back in his chair. The comfortable seat was in keeping with their luxurious surroundings. For Humphrey to select this club for tonight, he must be doing well with his own investments. As to the question of Perceval being an ally or an enemy, David sighed. Perceval was a complicated character; like most humans, he confused David with his lack of logical thought. It was wrong to own other humans, but wasn't it also wrong to tell humans who they might desire? Apparently not, according to Perceval.

"Surely you must know it's complex. He appointed half the commission who approve the loans for the Caledonian Canal—" The project was necessary to get a transportation link through the Highlands, yet here he was, sitting in some—admittedly lovely—club with his businessman Humphrey, listening to him make off-handed jokes when he should be doing his job and getting the funding for the Caledonian Canal fixed. His righthand man had an annoying habit of being not as serious as he ought to be. Yet, when the crunch came, he always managed to pull a solution from the hat. How? David was unsure. Some kind of wizardry—it certainly didn't appear to happen by any weight of proper work. As much as Humphrey's magical ways irritated David, he needed him because his ridiculous manner always found the finances David required. Results mattered, not the method. If only the method wasn't so illogical. He didn't understand how it worked and that infuriated his engineering mind. Ten years and he still hadn't solved the puzzle of how Humphrey managed to be so continuously successful. He'd stopped trying to comprehend a long time ago.

"Yes, that is a rather contentious relationship." Only Humphrey could dismiss the whole mess as contentious and make it sound like it was a minor issue. The project's debt continued to accumulate, and they had little to show for it. Fancy expensive locks that were unconnected to the main canals. Boats could go up and down, but not towards anywhere useful. David breathed in deep and reminded himself that somehow in his own mysterious way Humphrey always managed to find enough money to get things built.

Therefore, if he must sit in a damned social club with Humphrey as part of his business partner's process, then he would grit his teeth and put up with it. It wasn't all terrible. The view was rather pleasant, especially the double bass player, who was the only man in the naked string quartet. The simple erotic way his bow stroked across the instrument drew attention to his superior form. David had a sudden urge to stroke the musician's forearms in the same rhythm. Unfortunately most of the musician's body was hidden by the double bass. His own imagination would have to provide the details, and with that realisation, he blinked. He needed to focus—or rather, he needed Humphrey to focus so he could continue his important work.

"Are you waiting for someone?" David asked. The way Humphrey kept glancing at the front door gave it away. Technically it wasn't the front door to the street. The club was non-descript from the outside, just another plain terraced house, and anyone entering would step into a small hallway with a concierge and a cloak room. Nothing gave any indication that the main door at the end of the hallway opened into a luxurious lounge room with deep sofas set into alcoves. It was designed for conversation, and possibly more, given the obvious hint that only a naked string quartet could give. One could hardly be more obvious that this was a den of sensuality.

"I... ahh—" Humphrey dallied, and David sneered at him.

"Why did you invite me here? I have plenty to do. More... Especially now, assuming the Prime Minister is dead."

Humphrey swallowed and stared at the front door again. Patches of colour spread over his cheeks. "It's Sutherland. I invited him."

"What?" David stood up, so quickly it felt like he left his stomach behind on the sofa. "No."

"I only want you to be happy." Humphrey's face paled and his gaze darted around the room.

"Is this one of your pesky schemes to distract me?" David pulled himself together with a deep breath and sat down again. He leaned forward and whispered. "I don't need Sutherland. I need the funds to complete my canal."

"But I thought you and Sutherland were..."

He'd never seen Humphrey so uncomfortable, and if he wasn't so off-guard himself, he would've questioned him about it. "No. Sutherland made it very clear that he couldn't cope with my commitment to my work. He wanted someone to be with him, not someone who spent most of the year travelling to inhospitable places."

"Oh. I'm sorry. I seem to have misunderstood."

David glared at Humphrey. "Yes. It's a nasty habit you have."

Humphrey hesitated for a fraction of a second, then deliberately placed his hand over his heart—a mocking gesture if David had ever seen one—and grinned. How he could grin when David had just had his heart trampled all over again by the mention of Sutherland, he didn't know. Humphrey's worst nasty habit was the perpetual way he did this; somehow reacting in an illogical manner that left David off-balance.

"Just ask the Luddites. It's not the only nasty habit I have."

"The Luddites?" David didn't have time for Humphrey's games, not right off the back of his comment about Sutherland. What did those close-minded old-fashioned thugs have to do with anything? He sipped his whisky only to find it already empty, so he waved at Mrs Skarsgard for another drink.

"How long have we worked together, David?" Humphrey shot him a look of pure disdain, leaving David wondering what he'd done wrong. "And you've never asked me about my family. Do you have any clue that my family, the Dexingtons of Manchester, run a linen manufacturing business? The news about Perceval... if it is true... will be a great shock to them. He was a key supporter of manufacturing against the Luddite movement."

"The Luddites need to understand that new machinery doesn't take away jobs, it just changes the jobs that exist."

"David." Humphrey shook his head. Right—if his family were in linen, then he hardly needed David's explanation of the Luddites and the way they tried to disrupt change by simplistic methods such as burning down buildings housing machines. Didn't they realise they were stopping everyone from employment when they did that?

"And here we are. Once more, I'm trying to do something kind for you, to get your close friend here so you can be happy before we both have to argue with the Loan Board and head to the Highlands to ensure the summer schedule is on track."

"You don't have to come." David focused on the easy part; ignoring Humphrey's attempt to help him sort out his ruined relationship with Sutherland. If Sutherland didn't want him, that was the end of it.

"Every year you say that and every year I come anyway. It is impossible to acquire funding without understanding the project. I need to know the progress, the difficulties, all the details so I can communicate effectively with our investors."

David swallowed. "I see." He didn't see. Not at all. With a pounding heart, he realised that he probably hadn't seen for a long time. Humphrey had always been there, by his side, championing his work, and now... Right now, when the Caledonian Canal project was an utter disaster, he was still here. Not only that, but Humphrey had tried to do something kind for him. Misguided, sure. How typical of Humphrey to get the wrong end of the stick in his attempts to help, and yet, David had no doubt that Humphrey truly believed it would be useful and kind to invite Sutherland here. The poet wouldn't show. They'd ended their affair on a nasty note, one that would be hard to apologise for. David refused to apologise for his work, and Sutherland refused to stop wanting more from him. David couldn't give Sutherland what he wanted, not without compromising his work.

"I'm sure you do." Humphrey shifted in his chair, turning his back on David, clearly annoyed with David's self-centred lack of knowledge about his businessman. Humphrey was right; they'd worked together for so long and David never bothered to ask Humphrey anything about himself. Provided he did his job and got David the investors he needed, he'd never given Humphrey another thought. Scratch that, it wasn't entirely true. He'd given up trying to understand the incredibly frustrating man and his illogical charm; he'd dismissed Humphrey as an impossible puzzle. One not worth his focus.

"Humphrey?"

He glanced over his shoulder. "Yes?"

"When you said this club caters to people like us, did you mean...?" He couldn't bring himself to say it aloud. Humphrey knew all about his affairs, so much so that he knew to bring him to a club like this where he'd be safe to love another man. And it made David realise that Humphrey was correct; David had spent over a decade of his life with Humphrey by his side and he knew nothing about the man. He'd treated him like a tool, one that he used to get what he wanted. Not like a real person. It didn't reflect well on himself as a person if he couldn't take a little bit of time to care for someone who always had his back. His chest continued to tighten, and he had an urge to loosen his cravat and make it easier to breathe. Humphrey was a loyal friend, more than a businessman who ensured David could achieve his goals. Humphrey worked in unexpected and confusing ways, and yet, one thing was true. He was always there when David needed him. Always. Faithful—unlike everyone else. And David hadn't seen him at all, hadn't valued his contribution for the simple reason that he didn't believe that Humphrey did anything solid to achieve it. But that couldn't possibly be true. No one had ten years of continual good fortune and lucky breaks. David felt like his world had been tipped upside down.

"David. My job is to notice things about people. I need to convince them that investing in your projects will give them everything they want—ergo, I need to understand what they want. I'm good at it." Humphrey confirmed that there was skill involved in gathering the necessary funds for his projects. They weren't skills that David had, hence his undervaluing of them, and he couldn't believe he'd made such an error for so long. "When I said this club is for people like us, yes, I mean men who don't want to take a wife, women who don't want a husband, people who might want both. In essence, the Soho Club is for everyone who can't be who they truly are when they are out in society. It's for anyone who doesn't quite fit into society's narrow band of acceptability. People that The Honourable Spencer Perceval and his devout pals found to be an antithesis of good manners. In other words, my type of people."

"But I've seen you with women…" David made excuses for his own lack of observational skills. He hadn't even credited Humphrey with the skills to do his own job properly, assuming instead that it was luck, or his handsome smile, that gave him consistent results over the last decade. Oh. He hated to make errors and this one felt like a clamp tightening around his chest. A clamp. No, a boulder crushing him flat so he couldn't breathe.

"I have seven sisters, David. They have friends. I happen to like women as people; they are often charming and more interesting than society allows them to be." Humphrey didn't quite answer the question David wasn't sure he was asking. Did he really want to know if Humphrey shared his desire for other men? It wasn't exactly the type of thing discussed in polite society; hence why clubs such as this one existed.

"Seven?"

"Yes. You are a capable engineer and by extension, good at arithmetic. It's not a difficult concept."

"I had no idea."

"I know." At some point in this revealing conversation, Humphrey had turned back to face David and he stared at him with those steel grey eyes that always seemed to see right through David. It was unsettling. It always had been. Which is why he'd ignored the way Humphrey looked at him for so many years. When they'd first met, David had been charmed by Humphrey, and he'd definitely noticed Humphrey's strong jaw, gorgeous smile, sharp intelligent eyes, and handsome body with shoulders that filled out his jacket without assistance. It hadn't taken long for the initial glow to fade as Humphrey treated David like he did everyone else. He'd replaced being charmed by him with a stiffness and distance that he wasn't sure he could undo because Humphrey's smile wasn't special for David; Humphrey looked at everyone as if they were the only person in the world. Perhaps that was the secret to his ability to acquire funds for their projects.

CHAPTER THREE

Humphrey had spent many years waiting for David to see him, to truly notice his capabilities. He'd assumed it would be satisfying. He thought it would make him happy. He'd been wrong. It was one thing to know that David only saw him as a tool to get his projects happening; and quite another to have it confirmed that David knew nothing about him. A loud ringing in his ears echoed until it hurt. He wouldn't give David the satisfaction of knowing he'd hurt him. No, this wasn't hurt. It was anger, like the heat of a forge swelling and glowing inside him.

"I know." He stated the truth. David continually overlooked him, underestimated him, and didn't see him. To have David realise this was not as fulfilling as he'd hoped.

"I need some time to think." David stood up and began to leave.

"Wait." Humphrey didn't want to beg and the strained note in his voice hung in the atmosphere as if Humphrey had tugged on David's jacket like a needy toddler. "We need to confirm the news about our esteemed Prime Minister and then decide on a strategy."

David turned back to him. "You are more than capable of sorting that for yourself." It never sounded like a compliment when David used that tone.

"David. Like it or not, we are a business, a good team. Let's do this together." Humphrey didn't only mean their business. He wanted to be with David as a proper couple, teamed up in all ways, but he'd basically given up on the idea years ago. This conversation was the final blow to Humphrey's hopes. He'd never have what he yearned for; David's attention.

"Don't push me now. I said I need to think."

Humphrey shot to his feet, tired of suppressing his anger. "No. You don't get to do this. You don't get to run away when it suits you. I've stood beside you for a decade, David. It's literally my business too, my name on the same documents beside yours, my risks. If there is any thinking to do, we do it together." He was tired of being taken for granted. The yearning to be seen by David hadn't gone away over the years, it had only grown, and now—just now—at the moment David almost saw him, well. How dare he run away? David simply stared for a minute, then left anyway.

Humphrey stood awkwardly and stared across the room at the door, at the space where David had marched through, away from Humphrey once more. So much for that. The musicians continued to play, and a few other groups of people scattered around the room kept talking, creating a background noise that hummed beneath the loud thud of his heartbeat. After a short while he realised that only he could hear the clamour of his heart. The others in the room were too caught up in their own considerations to care for a pair of men bickering over some fine whisky. He supposed he ought to be thankful that he hadn't made a full confession of his long term—he cleared his throat—um, fascination with David.

"Mr Dexington, are you well?"

"Yes." He lied to the middle-aged Indian woman who was tonight's Mrs Skarsgard. She wore a magnificent green and gold sari with real embroidery. None of the cheaper painted fabrics for her; he was sure the sari was made of the very best quality silk, making it an extraordinarily expensive garment. The club—run by a collection of widows who all went by the same name for some unknown reason—must be doing well financially. It was none of his business and everyone seemed happier to leave the Mrs Skarsgards alone with their reasons for anonymity.

"I've just had some difficult news."

"Ahh, the Prime Minister. Yes, a terrible business."

It wasn't what Humphrey had meant, however, it would suffice for now. Better that than admit the truth about how he felt about David. "Do you know anything further?"

"No. The evening newssheets simply said that someone walked up to him in Parliament and shot him. There aren't any more details. Can you imagine?"

"Not particularly. Perceval wasn't that divisive, not as far as Prime Ministers go."

The Mrs Skarsgard frowned. "I do hope it isn't someone with a wider grudge. What if others in government aren't safe?"

"I don't imagine that will impinge on your business much." Humphrey tried to deflect with a jest, because the idea of some rogue element—a French spy, or a Luddite with a grudge—wandering around London and shooting important people didn't sit well. They weren't in a penny novel set in the wild west of America. In London everyone kept up a pretence of civility, or rather they used manners as a shield for their often uncivil actions.

"It may or it may not. We are very discreet with our patrons."

"As it should be. Not all of us have the circumstances where we can lounge in your main spaces enjoying the entertainments." Humphrey smiled. "Thank you for your hospitality tonight. I must dash off. As usual, please send the bill to my address." He'd barely touched his whisky, and David hadn't had much of his second glass. A lesser establishment would discreetly pour it back into the bottle to reuse for another customer. Damn, Humphrey had stayed in some terrible inns in the Highlands while touring various projects with David. Only the superior Scottish whisky had helped make the rough accommodations tolerable. He couldn't help a little petty glee at the notion of Sutherland the poet upset at such places. Only one thing was more difficult than David taking him for granted, and that was watching the continual parade of short term relationships and lovers that David enjoyed. If he could figure out a way to stop loving David, perhaps he could also have an affair with someone. He wasn't completely inexperienced in matters of the body. He'd had a few heated evenings with men he'd met at places like the Soho Club. He'd never been able to commit to more than one night with someone because they weren't David. Why settle for someone else? It wasn't fair on Humphrey and it certainly wasn't fair to the man who could never be David.

Humphrey didn't see David for the next few days, and he kept himself busy by going to all the right clubs. Not the fun ones like the Soho Club. The stodgy ones where politicians ate lunch and mused over how to maintain their powers, and the ones where the old aristocratic men doled out favours to people like himself and David. He even managed to spend an afternoon at Whites, listening to Lordlings add ridiculous bets to the famed betting book, and listening carefully to gossip so he could find leverage. The financial world was a grubby place. He had to balance the morality of each individual against their desires; some of them could be swayed by the production of a troublesome son's debts so they could be paid off without troubling the gossips of society, others took a little more convincing to get them to part with funds for David's projects. The time was well spent, as he worked out the new lines of influence. The assassination of Perceval turned out to be a dull thing; a businessman with a personal grudge who'd admitted everything. The hard work lay in understanding the important questions around who took over, not the Prime Ministership but the sub-committees and lines of communication, and where the new power bases lay. It took focus and great listening skills to work out.

His apprentice, a young man of Jamaican descent with the unlikely name of Smythe, walked into his office.

Humphrey smiled, pleased to see Smythe, who had recently taken on more responsibility in the business, doing more than errands and basic computing like when he'd begun his apprenticeship three years prior.

"Smythe. Have you finished the background on Lord Hansberry that I requested?"

Smythe nodded. "I have a few minor details to confirm and will have it on your desk in a few days."

"Thank you." Humphrey's large oak desk had been his gift to himself with the bonus payment they'd had from the owners of one of their successful Welsh canal builds. He liked to keep his paperwork neatly filed in large drawers that lined one wall of the airy room. With large windows along the other side of the room, the space was light and easy to work in during the long winters when Humphrey wasn't travelling with David to various sites.

"Mr Mattson is here to see you."

"Excellent. Show him in." Humphrey tensed as Smythe left the room. After all these years, he still had to prepare himself for the first sight of David. His confident, nay, arrogant stance, and broad strong body. Every single time he saw him, he had to fight the urge to reach out and touch him. Any touch would do, a simple pat on the shoulder, or a brush of knuckles over his forearm. He shoved the feeling aside with the habit of many years and forced his hands to relax at his sides. David only wanted this piece of paper, not him. A bank draft written out to their engineering company for a sum that would pay their Caledonian staff for the next two years. Now they had acquired the funding, it was time to get on site and ensure the work progressed.

"Humphrey. You sent me a message?"

"Yes. I have secured the funds for the next two years for Caledonian, and I have confirmation from Sweden that they want to progress with planning for their canal project. It sounds incredibly challenging."

David's eyes flashed wide open, then slowly his face relaxed and he smiled. His smiles were rare, worth the hours spent listening to rich men talk about themselves incessantly as if they'd achieved success on their own and hadn't simply been fortunate to be born into generational wealth. Many of them were so overbred and spoilt, they couldn't dress themselves, and yet they wielded the money and power David needed to complete his projects.

"Sweden. I'm surprised, however, we have learned many valuable lessons in the Highlands which will prove to be the reason we can make Sweden a success."

"We?"

David blushed a little. Hmm, the unusual sight sent a rush of heat down Humphrey's spine. "I've come to realise that I couldn't have achieved any of my recent projects without your assistance. We are in business together and I ought to value your contribution."

Humphrey nodded, keeping his gaze low so he didn't blurt out the truth. It was all for you. "Thank you." He managed to croak out a response.

"What? No random comment and accompanying grin?"

Humphrey's head jerked up. "You finally notice my work after years of dedication and expect me to joke about it. No, a thank you will suffice."

"You think I'm selfish?"

Humphrey almost nodded and stopped himself. "No. I think you are driven to success. Your focus can often make you single-minded in your goals."

"Isn't that selfish in prettier words?"

This time Humphrey did smile. "Pretty words are my speciality. How else do you think I obtained this?" He waved the bank draft and waited for David to realise what it was. The satisfaction he thought he'd get when David finally noticed him, finally flooded in and warmed his torso.

"Is that?"

"Yes. I told you I'd gained the necessary funds."

"I thought you meant you had agreement, not that you had the bank draft in your hands. Why isn't it in the bank?"

"Details, David. I thought you would want to see it. We can take it there now."

David grabbed the bank draft from Humphrey's hand, his fingers sliding accidentally against Humphrey's knuckles, leaving a hot trail of sensation behind. "Come on."

Humphrey stood up and shook out his hand to get rid of the prickly feeling. It didn't work and he rubbed his knuckles with his other hand before he followed David out of his small home onto the street where they hailed a hansom cab to take them to Child's Bank.

CHAPTER FOUR

After a few days stuck in a cabin in a collier sailing up the east coast from London to Edinburgh, they'd stepped out in the northern city to meet with investors on the Caledonian Canal project and David had forced himself to attend the meetings he usually didn't bother with. He wanted to watch Humphrey at work because he couldn't figure out the puzzle of Humphrey's continual success without watching in him action. It was beyond time to figure out how he was so damned lucky all the time.

Humphrey had stunned him with his deep understanding of the broader issues; how the canal would make ship transport safer while the war with Napoleon continued, as well as how much it would reduce the amount of sailing time and distance for any boat that needed to travel around the tip of Scotland.

Now they were in a private boat, sailing to the locks at the top end of the project, and from there, they would go overland by horse, slowly inspecting all the works until they arrived at the large locks, dubbed Neptune's Staircase by locals, at the Glasgow end of the project. He'd spent most of today working on the plans for the Sweden project, mulling over the best way to navigate the terrain based on the survey plans he'd been sent. He really needed to see the location in person and work out best way to proceed.

"Do you think we could hire a ship to take us to Sweden?"

Humphrey looked up from the book he was reading. "Anything is possible with the right amount of funds."

"That is no sort of answer at all." They'd fallen back into their old routine where David asked sensible questions and Humphrey said ridiculous things that irritated him. His decision to pay more attention to Humphrey—for the sake of the business—wasn't going very well. Realising that he'd assumed Humphrey was lucky and not skilled had shaken David to his core. A good engineer understood the people who worked for him, with him, and knew the full extent of their capabilities. To have severely misjudged Humphrey because he was charming, bothered David immensely. He wanted to spend this tour of the Caledonian Canal changing the way he treated Humphrey. Damn, he made it so bloody difficult, though, because Humphrey was always joking whenever David wanted to discuss something serious.

"Will you accompany me to Sweden?"

Humphrey wrinkled up his nose and David held his breath. This could go in any number of random directions. "Oh, it's almost as if you enjoy having my company."

David growled under his breath. "Of course I do. You've been my constant companion for this last decade."

"Not entirely. You took Sutherland on the last tour of works."

"A mistake of grand proportions. He found the conditions of many of the inns beneath him and struggled to cope with the quality of the meals. Oh, bother. There was a long list of complaints."

Humphrey didn't grin, as David expected. "I sympathise with the poor man. I'm sure he thought he was going on a grand tour with you to spend his time lounging around in lovely old manor houses being entertained by various people of note. And instead, he ended up with a man obsessed with his work who barely notices what he eats or where he sleeps."

"Is that how you see me?"

"You ask that as if it is a problem." Humphrey winked at him, and the grin David had been anticipating finally broke free. He really was charmed by Humphrey's smile, the way it stretched his cheeks and how his eyes squinted at the corners leaving deep wrinkles that somehow added to the joy. How a hint of his crooked teeth showed against his bottom lip, and for the first time in a decade, David let himself enjoy the little shimmer of lust that came with the smile. It had been years since he'd let himself wonder what Humphrey's lip would taste like. Damn it. This situation with Sutherland had left him without a lover for too long. He was seeing things and feeling things he ought not feel. How illogical that he might be reminded of his initial lust for Humphrey, a lust he'd buried for a decade for the sake of work, now that he'd finally realised that Humphrey was a solid business partner who knew what he was about. A handsome man with a wonderful smile, and the way his eyes glinted as if he believed in David wasn't easily ignored. Now he'd broken the habitual suppression, David had the unnerving sense that he'd opened a lock and water poured through until he was taken along with it, unable to stop.

"You don't think my work habits are a problem?"

"No. I admire your commitment. I wouldn't have dedicated a decade of my life to ensuring your work had the necessary funds if I didn't believe that you could achieve the impossible. No one else could create a canal through the Highlands."

"It is taking a rather lot longer than I'd hoped." An understatement if there ever was one. Four years into the project and none of the sections were joined into a cohesive canal yet.

"Only because you have faith in your own abilities and you overestimate what is possible because you assume everyone is as good as you. Of course you thought you could simply finish this one with ease and progress to the next project. The fact that it's been a challenge is a good thing."

"How so?" David wasn't sure he wanted the answer. He scoffed at himself. If that was true, he ought not to ask the question.

"I've seen how irritable you get when you are bored."

"Oh that is not true." His retort held a note of uncertainty and he sent Humphrey a brazen look to try and counter it.

Humphrey raised one eyebrow. "Are you certain about that?"

"It is true that I don't like it when I'm forced into a dull situation, but I don't get irritable." David glared at

Humphrey, as a flush of irritability rose in his chest. If Humphrey didn't continually nag at him like this, he'd be rather a good chap. "Damn you."

"Now I know it must be true. You've resorted to insults."

David had no response to that nonsense. He blinked, forcing himself to hold Humphrey's gaze as his businessman stood up with one hand raised up. Humphrey's eyes danced with good humour.

"Surely you must know yourself enough to realise that you only insult me when I'm right and you are wrong." Humphrey's mouth quirked up at one corner. If it wasn't for Humphrey's palm between them, David would've leaned in and kissed Humphrey on his cheeky blasted smile to stop him from this incessant teasing. "Do stop glaring at me, David. Me being right has occurred on a few occasions in the past decade."

David gaped at him as the glow in Humphrey's eyes took away the last semblance of good sense he had remaining and he marched over to him. He pushed Humphrey's hand to the side, leaned closer, and kissed him hard on that damned cheeky mouth of his. Shock rocked him. Oh damnation, David was going to hell in a handbasket. How had he been so obtuse as to not notice Humphrey for all these years? The subtle taste of him—toothpowder, tea, and a hint of bacon— as their lips touched, and the prickle of his stubble against David's softer moustache, all combined in a rush of lust, hot along his spine.

Humphrey, of course, reacted in the most unexpected fashion. David assumed he'd be rejected and pushed away. What kind of person kissed his businessman without warning? But Humphrey wrapped his large hands around David's face and pulled him closer. He kissed David as if he'd been waiting a decade for this moment and he wanted to savour it; the kiss wasn't desperate or needy, it didn't reflect the surge of hunger inside David. It was better than his own desires. Better than anything he could have hoped for. It was a homecoming; a welcome, and every stroke of Humphrey's tongue became a moment David hadn't known he'd needed. There was something special about being kissed as if he were a delicious treat that Humphrey had dreamed about for a long time. Humphrey savoured David. There was something incredible in the way he gently nibbled at David's bottom lip, all the while cradling his face. David had never been kissed like this, as if he mattered, and even though he'd started this, he could barely continue because all his breath had been stolen by the sheer wizardry and beauty of Humphrey's mouth against his. David let himself drift into the sensation of it, the impossible wildness of Humphrey who always, always surprised him. He pulled back.

"I'll never be bored with you." He didn't give Humphrey time to reply because he hadn't meant to voice his honesty out loud. Perhaps the reason he was continually irritated by Humphrey's chaotic manner of business was because he was trying his best not to recognise this ferocity between them. Maybe he was always irritable with Humphrey because he was tired of the pretence that this didn't exist. He covered Humphrey's mouth with his own and tilted his head so he could stroke his tongue over Humphrey's own. Someone groaned and the vibration went all the way into David's chest. He wrapped his arms around Humphrey's spine; one hand on his trousers to pull them together, and the other resting lightly on between his shoulder blades. Humphrey kept his hands lightly on David's face, as if holding him was a precious moment, and all the time, the kiss continued until neither of them could breathe.

"Holy hell." Humphrey twisted away, his voice ragged, and David let him go. He waited as Humphrey leaned his forehead against the cabin wall, his arm slung over his head. Humphrey's body stretched out, lean down his spine, and the cloth of his trousers stretched across his tight buttocks.

"I could fuck you right now and it would be amazing." Apparently an incredible kiss stole his ability to filter himself. His voice sounded odd, rough, and breathless, as if he'd spent a day working in a dusty pit.

Humphrey turned around, his cheeks ablaze. "You wouldn't."

"Why not?"

"I deserve more than one cheap rutting on a barque." Trust Humphrey to say something that made David's head reel.

"I can't give you more. All I'm good for is a quick affair between projects." David had been told this so many times that he believed it. Everyone, eventually, got tired of his commitment to his work and left him. He didn't dare take the risk that Humphrey would be the same. The business, his work, wouldn't survive without Humphrey.

"I want more than that." Humphrey stood up straight, stiff and tense.

"You do?" David didn't know how to separate his need to keep working with Humphrey from the insistent hardness in his cock. He had to because people didn't stay for him, and without Humphrey, his work would be much more difficult.

"So that's it then?"

David wanted to scream No. For a kiss like that, he'd pretend that he could offer Humphrey forever, except this was Humphrey. His businessman. "I'm sorry. It's all I have." How inconvenient to realise Humphrey's worth at the same time he rediscovered his lust for the charming handsome man.

Humphrey nodded, all the colour stripped from his face, and he walked out of the cabin door. A sharp fresh breeze blew inside before the door shut again, leaving David alone with his unsettled thoughts and thumping heart. He plonked himself down in the lone chair at the small table in their cabin and ruffled through the papers he'd spread out earlier. All the plans meant nothing without Humphrey by his side. When had he become so necessary to him? Together they achieved great things with many wonderful projects built. An old mentor had once told him that a great project manager is invisible. No one will notice a good job because the job gets done. It is only the terrible managers that create noise and fuss and problems.

David hadn't seen Humphrey's skill as a business manager because he simply got the job done. There was always money to pay for workers and for materials. Even on a disastrous project like the Caledonian Canals, Humphrey still managed to pull a rabbit from his hat and keep the whole thing afloat. David shook his head, hard, as if he could get rid of the overwhelming sense he'd made a terrible mistake. It wasn't luck, it was brilliant management. And now the Caledonian Canal wasn't the only disaster he was responsible for.

He'd made a mess of their functional business relationship. Humphrey was right. He deserved more than David; David who pushed people away when they didn't fit in with his plans. At near-on two score years old, David knew he would always put engineering before a lover. Humphrey must recognise it too; that David was a selfish brute. Humphrey was right to reject him. If only it didn't feel like he'd been hit with a shovel in the chest.

CHAPTER FIVE

The wind blew briskly into the sails of the barque. Humphrey stared out at the grey sea, letting the breeze sweep over his face. Salt spray whipped up off the North Sea and stung his cheeks, making a decent attempt to cool Humphrey's heated face. He'd had everything he'd yearned for in one moment, one kiss. It hadn't been enough.

He shook his head at his own damned pride. It would've been so easy to stay, to keep kissing David, because the kiss was almost everything he wanted. Was it selfish pride, or greed, that made him leave? David wasn't ready to give Humphrey forever; he'd made that more than adequately clear. A curse escaped his lips and was snapped away by the wind. If this wind kept up, they would make excellent progress and arrive in Inverness on the right tide. They'd pushed hard from Edinburgh with decent winds yesterday, and the early start this morning, meant they should arrive mid-afternoon. If not, they'd have to anchor and wait until the tide changed so they could access the lock. It was one of the engineering difficulties at this end of the canal that David hadn't found a solution for; a canal needed water at the correct levels, and the changing tides made the entry difficult. Waiting. Humphrey had already waited, impatiently, for over ten years for David to notice him. Now he'd stepped over that hurdle, could he risk waiting again? On a shuddering breath, he knew he had to. Neither himself nor David ever settled for a second rate job at work. A relationship would be the same. They both had to strive for the outcome they needed.

The kiss had been more than he'd ever imagined and yet, he valued himself enough to push David away. Cold air tingled his lungs as he breathed in deep. His instincts were right. He wanted everything; an extension on the relationship they already had. Steady companionship. Love. It wasn't enough for David to see that he was there. He wanted David to see that they would work well and be good together. What a damned fool he was to push him away. Stubborn pride, that was all. He wanted David to love him back with the same intensity that he gave to his engineering works. Humphrey blamed the wind for his wet eyes, blinking hard as he stood on the front of the barque. He let the wind whip around him until his cheeks ached with the cold of it. Scottish summers weren't much to write home about. Elspeth, his closest sister, a year younger than him and a considered spinster at twenty-seven, would want all the gossip about David and, besides, writing to her always helped clarify his thoughts. He'd pen her a letter tonight.

"Come inside and have a Scotch. You look frozen." David's stern instruction jolted Humphrey from his admittedly circular thoughts. The barque had docked a short time ago. Humphrey had lost track of how long he'd stood on the front of the boat, staring at the ocean, caught between regret and desire.

"I am, rather." He rubbed his gloved hands together and followed David off the boat, along the rough stone path, and into the tiny inn at the base of the partially completed Dochgarroch locks. The inn was little more than a stone building with a stable at the back with one horse and buggy for hire. Humphrey only knew about the horse, an overgrown pit pony, because he'd stayed here in four of the past five years while inspecting the works. Last year, he'd stayed in London while David took bloody Sutherland on his annual tour. For six weeks, Humphrey had tried to distract himself from the knowledge that David had preferred to take a lover on his annual tour, not his businessman. It gave him almost no joy to hear that Sutherland had found life on tour difficult; hmmph, well, that wasn't true. He did feel a little petty warmth inside because, unlike Sutherland, no conditions were too rough for him to cope with. He wasn't a soft poet who would put his creature comforts above being loved by David. Swallowing down the urge to let out a deep sigh at his own ridiculousness, he followed David inside, ducking his head instinctually to fit under the low eave of the door frame.

"McLoughlin. A couple of drinks please."

"Mr Mattson and Mr Dexington. How delightful to have you both back in our part of the world." The inn owner, barkeep, and general man of all work was a brash red-headed Scotsman with a deep brogue. Whenever they stayed here, Humphrey was glad he lived in London where he was accustomed to hearing accents from all around the world because he could understand McLoughlin without too much effort. London was the world's largest port, and people from everywhere passed through there, besides, he'd grown up in Manchester and his family's business had many trading ties to other parts of the world. Understanding people was one of his skills; more complex than simply listening carefully to their accent, although that was often a large part of it when dealing with traders from afar. People always responded better when paid the respect of being listened to. Although he might have described it that way for David or anyone else who asked, it wasn't as clinical as that. He just liked people.

David's jaw tightened a little. "Thank you. I would rather be travelling through." David referred to the uncompleted locks. Once done, they would likely sail right past McLoughlin's inn and continue to the end of Loch Ness. The barman frowned and Humphrey smiled quickly before McLoughlin gained the wrong end of the stick from David's unthinking comment. Project first was his focus and not many people understood his perspective, which led to a few misunderstandings.

"We always enjoy your hospitality, McLoughlin. Please forgive Mr Mattson for his terse lack of manners. This project is a great cause of stress for him." Humphrey bestowed his widest smile on the barkeep and when he smiled back, Humphrey's frozen cheeks began to warm up.

"We also have hoped the locks would be finished soon," McLoughlin said.

"All those promises of more customers will be kept. I shall see to it myself." Humphrey knew that once this project was done, more boats would use the whole canal and need places to stay on the more than sixty-mile journey. McLoughlin nodded tersely and slid two mugs across the wooden counter, one to Humphrey and the other to David who stood silently beside him. Humphrey picked up one and sipped at it. The excellent Scotch whisky slid down his throat leaving behind a trail of delicious heat.

"You've outdone yourself this year, McLoughlin. This is truly excellent."

"It is the same one we served you last year."

"I didn't come last year. Mr Mattson had a different companion." Humphrey sipped the Scotch again and it burned away the nasty bitter taste. Jealousy. It could only be. Well, he was here, and Sutherland was not, and neither of them had any chance of capturing David's heart. All he cared about was his precious locks. Another sip of whisky didn't get rid of the bitterness. Damnation, was he envious of David's work? Surely not. McLoughlin glanced quickly at David, the movement so slight, Humphrey doubted whether he'd seen it.

"Yes, I remember him. A pretentious chap who spent most of his time staring at our hills and saying odd things."

"Sutherland is a poet. He wrote some spectacular verse while here last year." David picked up his mug and skulked off towards the fireplace where he sat down and stared into the flames.

"Spare me from brilliant men and their foibles." Humphrey rolled his eyes deliberately and McLoughlin barked out a laugh.

"We have missed you, Mr Dexington."

"Thank you. I have missed your whisky and your very cosy rooms."

"You always were so kind."

"Am. I am so kind and it's the truth."

McLoughlin topped up his mug with a slosh from the bottle and waved him over to the fireplace. "Go and cheer up the surly engineer. The missus has made rabbit pie. I caught the rabbits myself this morning, so it's nice and fresh. I will bring some over shortly."

"Excellent." Humphrey went and joined David by the fireplace. He leaned in close enough to catch a hint of the nutmeg and tobacco scent that David favoured. "It is unlike you to take your stress out on a kindly barkeep."

David didn't answer, only sipped his drink again. Humphrey leaned back in his own chair and crossed his leg over his knee. He knew the casual pose would irritate David; perhaps enough that he might say something. He waited, slowly savouring the whisky, and with each sip, his cold body began to warm up. The fire flickered and danced, mesmerising as it tried to warm the room. There was something elemental about sitting in front of a fire; something that drew him towards the flame as it represented the beginning of human achievement. Together with David, they were creating giant structures that would change the way people moved around their part of the world; speeding up transportation of heavy goods and making transport safer to boot. Yet none of it could've been done without some person, a long time ago, figuring out how to capture and contain fire.

"Fire is such an unlikely tool." He gave up on trying to taunt David into a response. It was a boring game, and one he'd never won at before. He may as well share his chaotic thoughts.

"Spare me the philosophy, Humphrey."

He couldn't ignore that surly nonsense. "Think about it. Without it, the world wouldn't have metal works or warm houses or steam boilers to run the pumps used in mining. At some point in human history, someone decided to try and control fire. They took it from a scary natural phenomenon and realised that it could be used to keep them warm, cook food, and even create things. When you really think about it, it's pretty amazing."

"Are you going anywhere with this?"

"Do I have to? Not every discussion has to have a purpose. Sometimes the purpose is just to play with ideas and—"

David interrupted. "I doubt that philosophising about fire is going to help me get our work crews to finish the job faster."

Humphrey snorted. "Paying them in coal so they could light fires might though."

"Humphrey. Leave a man in peace, would you?"

"No. I don't think I will. Another drink?" Humphrey stood up quickly in a pretence of enthusiasm. After a short discussion and refill with McLoughlin, he sat down again and handed David his mug.

David took a sip and stared into the fire. "I don't understand you, Humphrey."

"For someone who spends their day imagining how a place will look once you've built something, you are rather terrible at ordinary observations."

"What do you mean?"

Humphrey sipped his whisky. "I don't know anyone else

who could stand on the edge of a valley and declare that if a bridge was built from one location to another, it would be possible to have a canal with a three degree fall."

"I'm not talking about engineering. If it was as straight forward as finalising a route through uneven terrain, then I'd already understand you. Other people aren't as tricky as you."

Humphrey shook his head. "I'm not a mystery. The only mystery is that you haven't paid me any attention until now."

"That is not true. I'm not talking about your work. I don't comprehend how you can shift rapidly from reminding me to be kind to people, then bounce right into a random discussion about fire. How are those things connected?"

"I take it you don't want the specific answer to that question." Humphrey paused, then with a short huff of breath as he waited for David not to respond, he continued. "They are related because I was thinking about how your stress regarding the work here impacts on the people around you, and generally thinking about work while sitting in front of a fire lends itself to a natural exploration of the nature of fire and how humans took fire and created all these things, and how your work here is a legacy, or a consequence, of those early actions by someone's ancestors."

"I... That's very creative of you."

Humphrey scoffed. "My father always said I was too creative in my treatment of the books. Maybe he was right, or maybe he was wrong, but look what we've achieved together."

"Wait." David twisted in his chair and Humphrey held his breath. He'd rather be quizzed on the reference to playing with the accounts than have David notice he'd mentioned his father for the first time since they'd met.

"Nothing I do with the business's finances is illegal." He kept his voice as light as he could, because even though it was the truth, a weight pressed on his shoulders. On occasion, he'd been a little creative; not exactly crossing any lines of legality, but he'd definitely taken some financial risks that David wouldn't be comfortable with. Besides, the law wasn't always moral, so it was hardly a guide for doing the right thing.

"I'm certain that's true. I have a different question."

Humphrey forced his jaw to relax and he gulped a large mouthful of whisky. It burned his throat, exactly what he needed, and he almost coughed to distract David. A different question was good, unless it was...

"I didn't know you had a father. You've never mentioned your family."

Humphrey swallowed a sigh. Unless it was that question. "That's not true. I mentioned my sisters only a short while ago."

"Two weeks. And until then I had no clue you had any family. You simply arrived from nowhere, with no references, and convinced my then-businessman to let you become his apprentice. Soon, you'd pointed out his errors, resolved a major problem with funding, and in less than a year, you'd taken over from him."

"Oh, old Rogerson was well past being able to do the work you required with any level of competence. He was fine for smaller projects with fewer variables. I'm surprised it took me so long to point that out." After all, Humphrey had learned accountancy from infancy on the knee of his father as he taught him how to manage the family business. It was only at Elspeth's insistence that Father taught her too, and for that Humphrey would always be grateful.

"You must have had some financial experience before you started work here. But you were only in your early twenties?"

"Eighteen." Technically, he'd not turned eighteen until three months after beginning work for the private company which had employed David to build a canal from the middle of Wales to the port at Cardiff. Now ten years, and a few months later, here he was, astounded that David not only knew nothing of his background but that he had never bothered to enquire about it.

"We were both so young. I was only twenty-six and had recently finished a stone building for Lord Monaghan. He took a big risk on asking me to run that project for him."

Humphrey wanted to roll his eyes at the way David framed himself as young when he had been only a couple of years younger than Humphrey was now. But the age gap paled in comparison to the dismissive way David spoke about his work. It wasn't just any stone building David had designed and constructed, it'd been a massive public building in Cardiff. Back then David's spectacular rise from stone mason, to foreman, to project director and chief engineer had already been well documented in the papers, and when Humphrey had needed a job and a new life, he'd chased the chance to work with David because he'd wanted to attach himself to a rising star.

"He obviously saw your abilities." As Lord Monaghan ought to, for David's engineering capabilities were patently obvious to anyone with a half-decent skill in observation.

"I was already in my mid-twenties with solid experience

when he chose me. That's quite different from giving a green eighteen year-old the command of the entire project's finances. What experience did you have?"

Humphrey wished he didn't have to explain his history. He'd managed to spend the last decade pretending he had, in fact, arrived from nowhere. He delayed by drinking more whisky. The drop McLoughlin offered was vastly superior to anything he could get in London for a similar price.

"Does it have something to do with your father? Are you embarrassed that he bought you a job?"

Humphrey choked on his mouthful. "Trust you to come to the completely wrong conclusion."

"What do you mean? You were so young to be entrusted with a large project."

"Naturally you saw my rise to success and immediately assumed nepotism, not any skill of my own. No. Father had nothing to do with my employment, and even less to do with my move from apprentice to master." It wasn't quite true. Father had taught him everything he knew about money.

"People don't come from nowhere with that level of financial knowledge." Trust David to understand. The problem with brilliant people is they tended to see past the surface.

"My family has a large linen manufacturing business in Manchester; you will have guessed from my accent that I'm from that part of the world. From as young as I could remember, I've been taught how to run the business..."

"Because you are the only son with seven sisters."

"Yes. You remembered that detail." Humphrey shouldn't be this impressed by such a tiny thing.

"You've given me so little information about you."

Humphrey laughed, surprised. "Surely that doesn't mean that you've squirreled each tiny snippet away and kept them all. Dear David, I didn't realise you cared so much."

David's cheeks darkened. "Humphrey. Must you?"

He smiled. "Teasing you is one of my favourite occupations."

"I can understand how your background gave you a good grounding in business management..." David ignored Humphrey's joke but when he paused, Humphrey waited. Just in case David didn't ask the inevitable question.

"Why aren't you still helping with the family business?"

Humphrey closed his eyes. There it was. The big question that had an ugly answer. He could lie and tell David the same thing he'd told Lord Monaghan; that his father wanted him to get some experience in other businesses before coming back to the family. It was partially true—that had been part of the original plan—a way to ensure the family business remained viable through gaining outside experience. Innovation didn't come from always doing things the way they'd always been done.

"The truth is..." He hesitated. Even though this was David, who would likely understand because he also desired men, Humphrey had never said this aloud to anyone. "The truth is that my father banished me from the family after discovering that I'd kissed a boy."

Anger gathered in David's features, making him glower from inside. "I'm so sorry."

"I should have been more careful."

"You were young."

"Yes. If there is to be some excuse, that will suffice." Humphrey still grieved for the lost relationship with his father, in the small quiet moments in the early morning before the sun had risen and the world was peaceful. If only he'd been more careful, with less youthful arrogance, he could've hidden the truth from his father, and he'd still have him in his life.

"You don't have to forgive him. He is the one who has made a bad choice. He made this decision."

"Thank you." Humphrey's heart ached; for David who saw enough to know Humphrey didn't need to forgive Father for his decision to throw Humphrey away like trash, and for his father who would never realise what he'd done. For himself too, because he didn't deserve to be tossed aside by his father simply for a desire he had no choice over.

CHAPTER SIX

David shouldn't be surprised at Humphrey's story; it was common enough among his acquaintances and former lovers. Some parts of society had a more open view, and he'd sought those out. Over the years, he'd also realised that many people—such as the recently deceased Prime Minister—were willing to overlook certain 'deficiencies of character' (as they referred to it) provided his work was better than good. It added to the puzzle that was Humphrey. How could he be so friendly to everyone when someone he cared for had been so callous to him? How could he continue to like people generally when his own father banished him from the family and his life so easily?

"In some respects, I am lucky," David offered. "Growing up it was just my mother and I, and she only wants me to be fed and happy."

"Fed? Was it hard growing up without a..." Humphrey paused.

David cut through the awkward pause. "Naturally it was

difficult to grow up in a small village with a near-blind mother, relying on the charity of others. Mother couldn't do mending or other small jobs to earn an income. I had a few father figures in the village who helped us out; I still write to the school teacher Mr Little every week and he reads my letters to Mother."

"She must be very proud of you."

"Mr Little certainly says so in his responses." David always wondered if Mr Little fudged the truth so it sounded more positive than reality. He hardly ever found time to visit the small village of his upbringing. It was tough to see Mother's decline; although it was obvious the money he sent to her was being used for her comfort. There was a measure of relief in knowing she was well cared for by those he paid. She said she wanted him not to worry about her and go on with his work. All he could do was his best for her.

"As you say, you are lucky." Humphrey lifted his mug up and McLoughlin came over to refill them both.

"The pie is almost ready."

"Thank you." David enjoyed Mrs McLoughlin's pies. Sutherland hadn't been pleased with the simple fare and it'd meant an awkward evening. "Please pass on my regards to Mrs McLoughlin. I always enjoy her meals." The barkeep nodded briskly and left them alone.

"There's a strange mystery there. This is a tiny inn and I've never met Mrs McLoughlin." Humphrey kept his voice low.

"It's no mystery." David chuckled. "There is no Mrs McLoughlin. I'm not sure there ever was. The barkeep does everything around here. I confess I'm not sure why he keeps up the ruse."

"Perhaps passing travellers feel more comfortable knowing their meals are cooked by a husband and wife team?"

"It's not really our business. The whisky is excellent, the food is filling, and it's always cosy and warm regardless of the weather outside."

"What are you saying?"

"Exactly what I just said. I'm here to work, and this place provides all I need to work properly. It's really not my concern how McLoughlin runs his inn." David didn't have room in his life to worry about trivial matters that he couldn't do anything about. He needed to make Mother's sacrifices worthwhile; to make her proud of him.

"Fair enough. Is that why you've kept me at a distance for so many years? I don't matter as a person, only as the skill I provide to your projects?"

David cringed at the partial truth. "Take care, Humphrey. That smacks of bitterness." The rest of the truth was that he cared too much for Humphrey; he'd just buried it deep. He should never have kissed him. It was like a leak in a dam's retaining wall; now they'd kissed, the leak grew stronger and all the feelings behind the dam threatened to burst out. He was a wall builder, not a wall breaker.

"Now who is deflecting? Why have you ignored me for so long?"

"Ignored? Are you jesting me?" David's ears burned. He had never ignored Humphrey—the very thought was impossible—but it wasn't the whole truth. "What nonsense. I've not ignored you." He had pushed his attraction to Humphrey aside, ignored it, pretended it didn't exist because it was damned inconvenient to care deeply for him. When they'd first met, Humphrey had been too young, and far too loud and assured of himself, and then they'd fallen into a routine of work.

"You can't deny the distance you've put between us."

"We work together. I won't put that at risk."

Humphrey raised one eyebrow. "Oh come on now. You kissed me. Without encouragement, might I add. So I know that's not the whole truth."

"Fine." David sipped his whisky to give himself a moment to collect his thoughts. It didn't help. He changed the subject instead. Damned if he was going to talk about kissing Humphrey while sitting before a cosy fireplace in a dark inn with a low ceiling. The atmosphere of the place invited intimacy. "I have no clue how you manage to succeed at your job and..."

"Hold on." Humphrey interrupted and held up one hand. "Are you jealous of me?"

"No." David cleared his throat and tried to keep his gaze firmly on Humphrey's piercing stare. "A little. You come armed with nothing but a charming smile and suddenly investors are giving significant funds to our projects."

"You think I'm charming?"

David turned towards the fire. "You know you are. You don't require my compliments."

"Well, thank you."

For a second, David thought he'd managed to distract Humphrey away from any personal discussion. He really didn't want to admit how he'd also been charmed by Humphrey's smile, by his friendly nature, and the way he looked at a person as if they were the most interesting thing he'd ever listened to. Over the years, he'd seen that look aimed at others and he knew he wasn't special to Humphrey. He acknowledged—at least to himself—that maybe he was jealous of how easily Humphrey shared his smile around. Obviously David wasn't special, and the smile wasn't his to keep.

"It's nonsense that you don't know how I do my job. You can't possibly be that lacking in observational skills. I've seen you at work, every little detail is worth your attention. The finances aren't a little detail." Humphrey's tone made it clear that he wasn't complimenting David.

"I'm not talking about the financial task of running the job."

"Are you sure? I've heard you say before that a good project manager should never be noticed. It's only when the job goes badly that people notice the project manager. It is exactly the same for the finances. When there is money to pay for goods, or labour, no one notices a job well done. It's only when the money runs out that people start screaming for a better manager. You don't see the work I do because you've never needed to see it. Even on this damned project, which is continually over budget and over time, we've never run out of money. I've worked bloody hard to convince investors to stick it out."

To hear his own thoughts repeated back at him should have been satisfying. It wasn't. David wanted to squirm in his chair, like a toddler who has eaten the last slice of pie and tries to lie to his mother with the crumby evidence all over his face.

"And I appreciate all your work over the last decade. Together we have done fairly well." David had managed to distract Humphrey from the key point; he understood the spending of the money perfectly well. What he didn't understand was how Humphrey managed to charm people into investing in the first place. Keeping Humphrey distracted wasn't as satisfying as it should have been.

"Fairly well? Bosh to that. You have incredibly high standards, David, and not only have I met them, but I've exceeded them to such an extent that even you don't realise it. I've cleared any bar you've set and freed you up to focus on the engineering itself."

"And that's why I keep you at a distance. I would never put our working partnership at risk with an affair." David muttered the last bit under his breath.

Humphrey chuckled. He'd clearly heard. "Oh, now you admit you've thought about an affair with me."

"Too many times," David mumbled, as he stared into the fire. Oh, McLoughlin's whisky had loosened his tongue too much tonight.

"One kiss and the dam breaks." Humphrey's tone teased him, more than he could know, with the same bloody analogy. David couldn't resist a glance sideways in case Humphrey smiled. Every single time. That damned smile sent a glow down his spine that he always struggled to resist. The whisky gave him the courage to stop resisting. How dangerous... Could he listen to his desires and put his entire livelihood at risk? No. Because people didn't stay with him for the long term and Humphrey would be the same as all the others. Eventually he'd get bored with being second fiddle to the job and he'd leave. David would be left without a lover and without a businessman. It was unconscionable.

"Smugness doesn't become you." David played Humphrey's own game and struck out at him. Again, it didn't give him the cheap thrill he'd been seeking.

"Oh? Are you suggesting that I've been right and you've been wrong twice in the past few days? Two whole times. My goodness. Whatever is the world coming to?"

"Humphrey," David growled. A warning or a need? Even he didn't know any more.

"Here you go, kind sirs. Fresh rabbit pie." The mouth watering smell of freshly baked pastry filled the air and David smiled gratefully at McLoughlin for his spectacular timing.

"Brilliant."

"Tell Mrs McLoughlin that she's out done herself." Humphrey waited until McLoughlin placed the tray on the small side table between them, then reached for a knife and fork and cut into his pie. Steam rose up from the pie and the scent of rabbit stew with a hint of some spice or other. David was glad for the food. It ended their uncomfortable discussion as Humphrey focused on eating. He was certainly not going to watch the way Humphrey's big hands held the sensible knife and fork, somehow making the crude country cutlery appear delicate. And he certainly wasn't going to watch Humphrey slide the forkful of food between his lips, lips he'd kissed and wanted to kiss again.

"Are you going to eat? This is spectacular. The use of Chinese five spice isn't something I'd expect in a small town in Scotland, but I suppose the spice trade has ventured further afield than London and Manchester."

"Yes." David blinked and wrenched his gaze away from Humphrey. He shoved forkfuls of pie into his mouth, not tasting any of it. He couldn't care about a discussion on food flavouring; food was for fuel and the time taken eating it often stopped him from working. If he were to give up some of his work time, he'd much rather be tasting Humphrey. Hmph.

"Why the sigh, David? The pie is outstanding. My sister's husband, Mr Chan, has a cook who uses these flavours and I miss it."

"The food or your sister?"

"Both." Humphrey rolled his neck on his shoulders, before tucking back into the pie. David could reach out and press his thumbs into the tight muscles at the base of Humphrey's neck. Or he could focus on the reason he was here. He needed to finish the Caledonian Canal and be a success. He wouldn't let Humphrey distract him. Aside from the weather and the issues with finding labour, the biggest problem was the terrain. The rocks were harder than he'd expected, the lochs not as deep, and in some sections they required dredging. If only Humphrey could be solved like an engineering problem, with a drawing, some mathematical calculations, and he'd have the answer he wanted. He chewed the pie more vigorously than it needed. The actual problem was that he was greedy. He wanted everything. Work success and Humphrey. He'd laid out the risks—too many times— and couldn't make it work because if things went wrong with Humphrey... and inevitably it would, given David's own record with relationships, then he'd end up with neither. He couldn't take that chance.

"That was excellent. Wholesome with a good blend of flavours I wouldn't have expected this far from the main trading ports." Humphrey wiped his mouth with a napkin and leaned back in his chair.

CHAPTER SEVEN

Several nips of whisky later, Humphrey's eyes were heavy with too much whisky and he'd spent way too much time relaxing in front of the fire thinking about David's kiss. He walked up the stairs to his small bedroom for the night and opened the door, only to stare at the lack of a bed. The room had a desk along one side, and a large easel set in the middle of the room with a half-finished painting of the locks on it. Ironic really, given the locks themselves were also only partially finished. He shook his head and headed back to the bar, nearly stumbling on the stairs.

"I think there is a mistake. There is a no bed in my room."

"Your room? You are sharing with Mr Mattson. We only have one guest room. The room you stayed in two years ago is now Mrs McLoughlin's art room."

"She exists?" Humphrey cursed the whisky for his loose tongue.

McLoughlin laughed, a quiet rumble that filled the room.

"Yes, she exists. My Mary is very shy, and it's been a big adjustment for her to live in the inn."

"Have you been married for long?" Humphrey couldn't remember when he first started hearing about the barkeep's wife.

"Coming up on three years now."

"She's been hiding for three years?" Damn, he really had had too much whisky.

"Hiding. You make it sound so mysterious. No, lad, she's just shy and she barely knows you."

"Fair enough."

McLoughlin grinned. "Her family moved to Dochgarroch from China when she was still in the classroom and we went to school together. It took me years to convince her to marry me. She was always worried that the inn would mean she would have to talk to people." There was such love in McLoughlin's voice, as if he would burn down his inn for her if she wanted it. He recognised the yearning because it was familiar; he'd felt it ever since he'd been a young apprentice accountant and had met David. He wiped the smile off his face as he belatedly realised he was grinning ridiculously at the memory of David marching into Mr Rogerson's office, wearing a mud smeared jacket and not bothering to introduce himself as he told Mr Rogerson what he needed. Humphrey doubted David even noticed him that day.

"People can be so difficult. I understand her reticence." Humphrey had seen the way people stared at his oldest sister's husband, Mr Chan.

"Thank you. She's always made the most beautiful paintings, and I promised her a room of her own to paint when we married. It's only because of your locks that I've been able to deliver."

"It is?"

"Yes. Every summer, we have an influx of workers for the new canal and they all like to have somewhere to have a drink and some food at the end of the day. Mary had the good idea of putting up tables outdoors, so we could feed more workers. They have their own accommodation, so we don't need to use both guest rooms."

Humphrey smiled, knowing that the men working on the canal stayed in temporary cabins they built for them, leaving the rooms in the inn for travellers. "I'm glad we could help." The flow on to the local businesses was a strong benefit of David's engineering projects, not just the long term effect of having the infrastructure, but also while they were being built. It was easy to forget that benefits while feeling so stressed about how long this project was taking. Speaking of stressed, now he had to inform David they'd be sharing a room. He cleared his throat to hide the flush of heat that slid down his spine.

"Thank you for bringing people here. When the locks open, more people will stop for a meal without staying the night. Mary will keep her painting room."

"I'm glad you could find a way to make it work for both of you. Please tell her I really enjoyed the pie. I'd better get Mr Mattson to his bed, since we have an early start in the morning." He emphasised the use of separate beds, just in case, because even though McLoughlin seemed like a good man, Humphrey couldn't be too careful. He glanced over at David and chuckled. The engineer was asleep in his chair. With a little awkward wave to McLoughlin, he marched over to David. It took a decent shake of his shoulder to wake him up, and he woke with a start.

"What?"

"Come to bed. It's late." Humphrey gulped as he realised what he'd just implied, right after being so careful. David simply nodded then stood up and stretched a little.

"Come on." Humphrey bolted up the stairs, again, struggling with the steep rises. He opened the door to the other guest room, and waved David through. Someone had put their cases in here earlier, neatly beside the two small beds.

"Sutherland hated it here."

Humphrey wanted to bury himself in the pillow. The last thing he needed was a reminder of David's former lover. "Hold on." Something occurred to him. "You call him by his surname even now."

"He preferred it. Insisted on it, in fact, because it was the name on the front of his books."

All of Humphrey's jealousy fled, and he doubled over in laughter. "How bloody arrogant. Oh, poor David, no wonder it didn't work out."

"Why not?"

"Two giant egos in the same bed. Come on now."

David's nostrils flared and he paced across the room to Humphrey. "You..." David stopped and kissed Humphrey rather than finish his sentence. Heat surged, as if the flames on the fireplace below had rushed up the chimney and filled the room with a blaze of fury. Humphrey kissed him back, holding nothing back. Every stroke of his tongue tasted like McLoughlin's superior whisky with that elusive hint of tobacco from David. A heady mix that made Humphrey sway with need. Desire lashed him, and he used his hands to touch David everywhere. Over his shoulders, down his spine, and under his jacket. He tugged, desperately, at David's shirt to pull it free from his trousers. He needed to touch skin. Now.

David rested his hands on Humphrey's arms, his fingers curled around his biceps. The kiss deepened, tongues and teeth and lips all pressed hard against each other, mimicking the way their hips ground together. Humphrey could barely breathe, and it didn't matter. He wanted everything. He finally got David's shirt loose and spread his hands over David's back. His skin against Humphrey's palms was exactly what he wanted. Taut muscles, hot skin, the combination was enough to make Humphrey swoon. Shit, he must be quite drunk. Men didn't swoon.

"Stop thinking." David's command centred him back into the moment.

"If only it were that easy," he mumbled and this time, David laughed.

"I can distract you."

"Please." Humphrey wished the noise in his head would go away. David's kisses were everything he had wanted for so long, and he still couldn't stop the silly comments. He ran his hands up and down David's back, across the hard muscles and hot skin. His shirt trapped him and David obviously felt the same as he growled and took a half step backwards. David grabbed his jacket and started to pull it off, leaving Humphrey no choice but release David.

"It'll be faster if I help."

David nodded and together they stripped the engineer of

his jacket and shirt. Humphrey slid the linen off David's shoulders and shook it out. The material, while good, wasn't as fine as the very best linens and he pushed away the memories of helping his father in their factory and learning about the different thread counts and quality. They imported most of their retted flax from Ireland and the treaty at the turn of the century had made the process easier, although better roads on this side of the Irish sea would help with transportation.

"What's the matter?"

Humphrey shook his head. "Nothing." He needed to stop thinking about Father's business. Those problems weren't his to solve anymore. Father had made that perfectly clear.

"Really?"

"Fine. Your shirt is linen. My family's business is in linen production. All this talk of my bloody father has got into my head, I suppose. Please distract me."

"My pleasure." David almost purred as he lifted his fingers to Humphrey's throat and began to undo his cravat with little tugs at the fabric.

Humphrey hummed low in the back of his throat. "My pleasure too, I think."

"Oh, most definitely."

Humphrey had seen David's flesh before; many times as they'd travelled together over the years in basic accommodation, but never like this. Never exposed for him. *For him.* He breathed in deep and his head almost spun. Too much whisky, or simply too much David. He wanted to touch him everywhere, kiss him everywhere. He'd waited so long, and he didn't want to wait any more. The first touch was hesitant, a palm against David's chest with his curly black hair slightly rough under his hands. David stripped off Humphrey's shirt and didn't hesitate at all. Soon, hands spread everywhere, all over each other, caressing until their breaths were fast and rough and trails of heat were scattered across Humphrey's skin. Humphrey jerked as David slid his hand down over Humphrey's hard arousal.

"More."

Sensation took over and Humphrey couldn't process all the details. All that mattered was David's hand reaching inside his trouser buttons and his fingers wrapped around Humphrey's length. Heat surrounded him and when the back of his knees hit the edge of the bed, he let himself crumple backwards.

"Please." This was better than his imagination could have supplied, much better than his own hand. He reached out for David, clutching his ribs helplessly as his own hips thrust hard into David's hand. "Oh fuck, I'm going to come." He squeezed his eyes shut tight. Not so soon. He had to wait, had to hold David too. David shifted, and Humphrey gasped as David's cock rubbed against his with David's huge hand holding them together. Sensation ruled. He buried his face in David's chest against the rough hair with a tang of sweat on his lips as he tasted David, kissed him all over his torso with an inelegant desperation. His hips bucked as he thrust against David over and over, and when he came, it was with a grunt that tore out of him with every jerk, until he collapsed, boneless. After a moment, he opened his eyes to see David's rare smile.

"What?"

"Why did I wait so long? You are glorious when you are utterly conquered like this."

Humphrey pulled David closer and kissed him hard. "I've always been yours." He spoke into the kiss, his drunk brain knowing he wasn't ready to admit that aloud yet, and the words disappeared into a tousled salty kiss that moved slow and deep and satisfying. David cradled the back of Humphrey's neck, comforting as Humphrey slowly drifted into a sated sleep.

When David woke the next morning with the sun streaming in the window, his head throbbed at the temples. He'd stayed awake after Humphrey had drifted off, taking his time to clean up Humphrey's mess, then had tucked him into bed before lying alone in his own tiny bed. He'd jerked himself off in a fresh handkerchief and fallen into a restless sleep.

"Mrs McLoughlin has made breakfast." Humphrey sounded far too perky given the amount they had drunk last night. "Damn. You look terrible. I will get you some willow bark."

"Thank you." He groaned as Humphrey slipped out of the room and closed the door gently. There was a damned good reason why he didn't drink too much; he had too much to achieve for lying around in bed all morning like a bloody poet. He hated the egotistical indulgence of it. This project was already behind schedule and he needed to get moving. It was time to talk to the foreman and get the project functional. He swung his legs out of bed, threw on some clothes, and marched downstairs with every step echoing in his head. The scent of bacon filled his nostrils. Yes. Just what he needed. He sat down at the table indicated by Humphrey and tucked into the hearty breakfast waiting for him. McLoughlin had outdone himself again with his superior hospitality.

"Here. Drink this." Humphrey placed a mug of thick black coffee in front of him and David sipped. Bitterness coated his throat and he almost gagged. He deserved this, so he forced himself to drink the rest down. Taste didn't matter; getting to work did.

"Now eat."

"You don't have to care for me," he growled.

"I know. But I want to."

David didn't have the strength to argue. He shoved the food in as quickly as he could manage without it threatening to come back up again, and greedily drank the glass of water Humphrey placed beside him. He ignored the way his heart thumped; not wanting to admit the truth. Didn't want to? Or couldn't? He had no clue; usually his affairs were discussed beforehand. One couldn't be too careful, and it made sense to outline expectations. This was new to him. A spontaneous evening; an amazing evening; but with so many pesky feelings of care left behind. He needed to pretend last night hadn't happened, because the truth was that he was only good for a temporary fling.

CHAPTER EIGHT

Humphrey wasn't sure what he'd done wrong that night. For the past week, David had woken before dawn and worked with the labour crew on site at Dochgarroch. Hard physical labour. Obviously, he was avoiding him. For the first few days, Humphrey had let him work. They were here to oversee this project and if David needed to get his hands dirty to achieve that, then it was simply part of his process. But after a while, Humphrey began to realise David was avoiding him. Over the years, they'd developed a rhythm when they arrived on these sites for inspections. David spent all day with the foreman and the men working on site, going over all the details, while Humphrey sat in a tent going through the accounts to verify the onsite situation against his own accounts. The foreman sent a letter every week with copies of receipts and costs. Being here was a valuable time to check for any discrepancies and, as with other visits, there was plenty of work to keep himself busy and distracted.

"If they keep up this rate of work, the locks will open at

the end of summer." David marched into the little tent that covered the foreman's office where Humphrey had spent the week working.

"I take it you are pleased?" Humphrey asked. They were scheduled to head across the Loch on a hired boat tomorrow towards the next worksite on the canal route, and Humphrey had already organised everything.

"We need to leave early tomorrow morning in order to get to the end of Loch Ness before dark." David's gruff voice gave no indication of any of the past week's lack of attention.

Humphrey nodded. "It's organised for daybreak."

"Good."

He wasn't going to ignore the way David had been working himself raw lately. "A day on a boat will do you good. You've been working too hard."

"I always work hard."

Humphrey raised one eyebrow. "Not like this."

"I'll see you in the morning."

"David." It was time to use his legendary charm to see if it would help him figure out what was happening inside David's head. He glanced around to check for other people, but of course no one else could fit inside this tent. Then he smiled as wide as he could.

"Yes?" David grunted and started to step out of the tent.

Humphrey then said the most outrageous thing he could imagine, purely to get David's full attention. "I think it's time we both played each other's bagpipes."

David stopped mid stride and spun around, taking a step back inside the tent as he glared at him. "Excuse me?"

Humphrey had to bite back a satisfied grin. "You've been avoiding me and there's only one conclusion to draw."

David's nostrils flared. "And what would that be?"

"You had the best evening of your life and you want more."

"How do you figure that from me not talking to you?" David's voice wavered with uncertainty and Humphrey's heart skipped a beat, but he was determined to find an answer to why David was obviously avoiding him.

"Obviously you are embarrassed to want me." Humphrey brazened his way through this with blatant nonsense. He had assumed David didn't want him, so he would tell David the opposite; just to get a reaction.

"I don't understand you."

"Oh?" Humphrey raised one eyebrow and attempted to appear quizzical. "What is there to misunderstand?"

"You accuse me of having a big ego and yet here you are."

Humphrey hummed a waltz under his breath and waited.

"Most people would assume that by me avoiding you, I'm avoiding wanting to have a negative confrontation with you. Most people would assume—"

"That you want me. Obviously."

David shook his head, then rubbed his eyes. "What? No. I rather think the issue is that neither of us want this. It was a drunken mistake."

"Now you dare to speak for my mind?"

David spluttered. "As if you haven't been doing that to me this whole time."

"Yes. That's exactly what I've been doing."

"Excuse me?" David's frown returned. "You are so bloody confusing."

Humphrey shrugged and spread his hands wide. "I'm confusing? I'm not the one who bolted from our room and spent..." He counted on his fingers. "Five days lifting rocks to avoid talking to me."

"I didn't."

"Now who is lying?"

"Fine. I did. We can't do this."

Humphrey paused, mostly for dramatic effect. He was being a toad to David. A deliberate choice and probably—no, definitely—petty revenge for the past five days. "Do you refer to our work, us not talking to each other, or the very pleasant interlude you've been avoiding talking about?"

"All of that. If we continue to indulge, we'll end up not working together and that would be an unmitigated disaster."

"I had no idea engineers were so dramatic. Ten years we've worked together. A few enjoyable drunken kisses aren't going to disrupt that." Humphrey was not as certain as he forced himself to sound.

"I'm not being dramatic. It's logic." David didn't even blink during his absurd retort.

"Logic? How so?" Humphrey pretended to appear quizzical with his head tilted slightly and the corner of his mouth tilted upwards. It was all an act, designed to draw more information out of David. A technique he'd honed over the years of working with David and his tendency towards a lack of communication.

"I've never had an affair last more than a season. People tire of my workload and they leave." There was a bitter note to David's whispered voice, but Humphrey ignored it for the bigger problem.

"Were you simply testing my resolve by ignoring me for these past five days? I believe I'm still here." He had been there for David for literally years. Not that David saw his commitment as real.

A small muscle at the corner of David's jaw flickered. "It's not worth the risk."

Humphrey closed his eyes and let all the air ease out of his lungs slowly as the joy of the discussion disappeared, only to be replaced with a sadness for the way David didn't believe anyone would stick around for him. "David. This is tricky for me too. I shouldn't taunt you like this about an obvious insecurity. Honestly, it's just because I have seven sisters and I'm used to talking about things when they are a problem."

"Is this what you call talking about it? Hassling me until I lash out."

"I've yet to see you lash out. Mostly you appear to be confusing me with someone else."

David shook his head. "Who? No, scratch that. What are you talking about?"

"You are confusing me with everyone else." Humphrey reached out to touch David on the shoulder, but he flinched away from Humphrey's hand and fled.

"I'm not going to leave, David." But the comment went unheard by David as he'd already departed the small tent, leaving Humphrey all alone to overthink his obviously poor strategic decision to taunt David rather than just tell him the truth. If only the truth didn't risk devastation when David rejected him.

The next morning, Humphrey sat beside David in the front of the small boat with the early morning sunshine shining bright off the lake waters. This part of the world was spectacular with the deep blue of Loch Ness and the sun painting the light stone walls of Urquhart Castle in an almost orange glow. The steep hills that lined the lake were a combination of schist, granite, and sandstone, all of which made the canal construction challenging, but Humphrey had to admit that the stark lines of the hills abutting the Loch were impressive in scale.

"Look, David. I was a bit out of line yesterday." He shouldn't have pushed David like that, especially without admitting his own desire for David first. David hummed under his breath but didn't speak and eventually Humphrey became tired of waiting.

"Don't you have a comment?"

"Is this what it's like having seven sisters? Do they talk at you constantly until your ears fall off with frustration?"

"Yes. I learned long ago simply to play their game." Humphrey laughed. "It's not the sister part that is noisy. I don't think girls talk any more than boys; probably less because they aren't supposed to talk or have opinions. It's more that there were seven of them."

"Hence you dominate conversations because they need to practice sitting around and looking adoring at your manliness?"

"David!" Humphrey grinned and a little swell of pride puffed out his chest.

"What?"

"You are learning how to offer ridiculous arguments. I like it. It's more fun to fight in that style."

"I'm not fighting you. You simply won't stop talking."

Humphrey chuckled. "And we haven't even talked about the most interesting question yet."

David shut his eyes and turned his gaze slightly away. After a few minutes, Humphrey's foot began to tap on the bottom of the boat. Even though he knew David was likely ignoring him on purpose, he couldn't resist. It was his greatest fault.

"Aren't you going to ask me; What is the most interesting question?"

"No. And I'm not inclined to let you tell me either."

"Damnation. You are no fun."

David's head flicked towards him, and his eyes glinted. "We are here for work. In my experience, mixing work with pleasure never ends well."

Humphrey wished he could take back everything he'd said yesterday. He'd teased and taunted to try and find out what was troubling David. The answer—that David viewed them as colleagues not lovers—was not satisfying.

"Sutherland really left a mark on you, didn't he?" Humphrey whispered, not sure if he wanted the answer. Suddenly, it was obvious that David had been hurt, badly, by the poet and his expectations of last summer's tour. A few kisses weren't going to solve this.

"Sutherland was the last of many." David certainly knew how to cut Humphrey's heart into ribbons.

"And so you blame yourself because these weaker men couldn't cope with your life."

"Engineering is all about patterns. A pattern has emerged, and I won't risk our work when the outcome is predetermined."

Humphrey could've made a joke about how he was a better man, how he'd already been here for ten years wanting David's kisses. He didn't. Couldn't. Once David made a decision, it was near impossible to change his mind. It didn't matter that this decision was based on flawed data. He folded his arms across his chest and leaned back on the seat. No amount of joking and teasing would change David's mind. All he had, all he would ever have, was one precious night when they were both too drunk to be rational. He couldn't even force himself to believe that David had truly wanted him that night; they'd really had far too much whisky for any sensible choices. All his hopes that the whisky had loosened the tension between them, so they could move forward in their relationship were dashed. He'd had his night with David. That was it. Now he had to learn to be content with his memories.

CHAPTER NINE

Six long weeks later, David's tour of the Caledonian Canal works had been a success. He should be pleased, happy. They could report to their investors that finally the project was on track, and this summer would break the back of the worst of it. Instead of building a sense of contentment, he'd spent six weeks battling a growing unsettling sense that he'd messed things up with Humphrey, and by extension all of his work.

"The locals want to call these locks Neptune's Staircase." Humphrey, for all his faults, hadn't changed during the last six weeks. He'd continued to tease and frustrate David with the same regularity as he had for the past decade. It was almost as if that one precious night in Dochgarroch hadn't happened. And that was why David wasn't pleased; because nothing had changed when everything should have changed.

"I suppose that is their right."

"Would you like to know why?" Humphrey asked.

"I assume because Neptune was the God of water, and

they bring the sea and the lakes together?" David didn't care for the name. Romanticising the Greek and Roman Gods was in vogue and quite frankly the locals could call the locks whatever they wanted. If it was up to him, he'd name them after the numerical system he used to keep his plans organised. Logic dominated the way he named things; and these locks were part of a sequence of locks that created the entire Caledonian Canal. Apparently, there was no logic to the way people chose to do things.

Just like how Humphrey had managed to stay so normally upbeat during these past six weeks, while David spent all his days dreading their conversations, even the ones about work. Humphrey operated the way he always did; magically finding more money from seemingly nowhere to keep the project running. At every site they inspected, Humphrey requested small changes to the operations and would run David through an outline to show how the changes would positively impact the accounts. Everything was the same, except it wasn't. David had been watching Humphrey very closely, almost obsessively, more and more each day as the tour progressed. If he hadn't paid so much attention, he would've fallen into old habits and assumed Humphrey to be exactly the same as every other year they'd done this inspection tour. He chatted easily to everyone and had a smile for all. It was in the evenings when David noticed small differences. There were less stories, less tales of the people he'd met and the ridiculous things they'd done or said. A little less vibrancy. David missed the way Humphrey used to try and drag him out of his safe comfortable engineering zone.

Engineering had rules. People didn't seem to. It always took David a long time to work out why a person acted the way they did, and why they made the choices they did. Honestly, most of the time he didn't bother to take the time to understand someone. There was one solid reason why he wanted to figure out the puzzle that was Humphrey. The kiss —their kisses—had been planted in his chest like a seed and it'd slowly grown into a sapling that wrapped around his heart.

"Is everything fine between us?"

"Yes."

"I mean, after that night in Dochgarroch, we are still able to work together?"

Humphrey blinked once, then gave him a hard stare. "It's been six weeks since you decided that we shouldn't revisit that one night. And suddenly you want to ask that question now?"

"I'm concerned about our work." David regretted bringing up the topic and tried to undo the urge to ask Humphrey about that night.

"I think you are lying."

David opened his mouth to protest, then shut it again. There was an element of truth in the statement. Trust Humphrey to be direct. As he looked around—anywhere but at Humphrey—he saw people everywhere. Busy people creating, working hard to put his plans into stone. "I only want the work to continue." He couldn't bring himself to admit the whole truth.

Humphrey shook his head with none of his usual smile and certainly without the glint in his eye that David expected to see. He walked off, leaving David to stand alone on the edge of a rock wall. He deserved that. A coward who couldn't admit he wanted Humphrey for more than his financial acuity and personable charm. He wasn't sure how long he ended up standing there, his mind unhelpfully blank.

"Mr Mattson. Excuse me." One of the stone masons walked up to him, waving an envelope.

"Yes?"

"This just arrived by collier for Mr Dexington. It's marked urgent. Where is he?"

David shook his head. "I'm not sure. Presumably in the overseer's tent?"

"Can you please find him? I'm required to help unload the new stones, and the boss told me to do this quickly then return."

David held out his hand for the envelope and nodded. He took the crisp paper with Mr Dexington written in curly handwriting on the front. The directions were vague; only to take the envelope to the overseer at the Caledonian Canal project and they would be able to find him. URGENT was written in capitals across the top of the envelope in slightly shaky writing. He marched along the rock wall towards the overseer's tent to deliver the message, trying to ignore the way his pulse quickened. Urgent was never good.

David tapped his foot as Humphrey read the letter. It hadn't taken any time to find him because he was precisely where David expected; hunched over the accounts for this portion of the canal project, tapping his pencil along the side as he went through the details. How many times had David seen him doing this, and never realised that the details mattered to Humphrey too? He'd been so focused on himself and his own issues that he hadn't noticed Humphrey's contribution. He'd wanted to dismiss it as luck, a fluke, because he didn't want to tell himself the truth. Humphrey was loyal—to the job—and to him. His stomach squirmed.

"What does the letter contain?" David couldn't resist.

Humphrey glanced up. "Some good news and some bad. The good news, at least for your project although not for the man himself, is that Lord Hansberry was seized with a fit of paralysis and died a few weeks ago. His heir is likely to release the funds and land we need to finalise the mid-section of this project."

David wanted to applaud the engineering gods. "That is promising. I have every faith that you will be able to talk his heir into good sense."

"The bad news is that I have to go to Manchester." Humphrey's gaze flicked around the room.

"To meet the new heir?" David's chest tightened. The one thing he'd known would happen—Humphrey would leave him—was coming true right before his eyes. Something odd grew his chest; was it relief that it was happening just like he knew it would? It had to be. Otherwise it might mean that he really cared and desperately wanted Humphrey to stay. He lifted his chin. Naturally, he wanted Humphrey to stay. It wasn't personal—surely? No, it was simply what it always had been; about the work. He couldn't afford for Humphrey to leave him, not now when the project was finally looking like it was going well. Not ever.

"No. A family matter." Humphrey's voice dripped with exasperation and David frowned. He didn't understand what was happening. Perhaps this twisting inside his stomach was simply hunger. It had been a while since he last ate. Difficult problems often had simple solutions. The trick was in seeing it. David needed to eat, that was all.

"Relax, David. I'm not leaving forever. I'll be back in a few weeks."

David breathed out in a rush of hot air. Humphrey would return. Of course, he would. Of all the people in David's life, Humphrey had been a constant for over ten years. He'd stayed while others had come and gone. With a gasp that released all the tension in his shoulders, he knew. David had been wrong, so very wrong, about Humphrey because Humphrey still promised to return. It wasn't food he needed to resolve this unsettled toil in his stomach.

"I will come with you." David never made quick decisions without considering all the options, except for now. He knew he needed to do this; to prove to himself and to Humphrey that he'd be there for him as much as Humphrey had always been a constant in David's life.

"What about your work?"

"My work can wait. We are a good team, and that means we should support each other. For over a decade, you've been there, assisting me in getting my projects delivered. You've never asked for anything. I rather think it's time I did something for you." And more than that, David wanted more kisses. He wanted more than an affair. For once in his life, it seemed possible that someone might love him and want him and stay for him. He'd yearned for someone to be his companion, his lover, and the very air he breathed. How ironic that Humphrey had been there beside him the whole time and he hadn't realised.

"Once the collier is unloaded, we can board and take it back to Liverpool. There are many canal boats travelling on the Bridgewater Canal from Liverpool to Manchester that we can hire a space for the final leg of the journey. It's a long journey that will take time away from this project. You needn't come."

"I'm already decided. You know I'm a decisive person."

Humphrey narrowed his eyes. "In ten years, you've never made a decision this fast without considering all the risks and options."

"You don't trust my choice." It was more of a question.

"I don't understand your reasoning. Only this morning, you told me you only cared for our work. This is out of step with that statement."

David nodded, as a grim wave of realisation settled on his shoulders. Only actions would convince Humphrey now. He'd spent so long fighting against this attraction to Humphrey—six weeks—ten years—and now he had to stop swimming against an impossible current. For years, he'd called it jealousy. He wasn't envious of Humphrey; he didn't want to be him. He wanted to be with him. He needed to be as loyal to Humphrey, as Humphrey had been for so long.

"You were right. I was lying this morning." David expected Humphrey to smile and make a joke of it, and when Humphrey only raised one eyebrow and settled his gaze on David, his throat filled with roughness. He cleared his throat. "I was lying to myself. I have been for a long time."

"I'm sure that is uncomfortable for you. However, your timing is terrible. I need to get to Manchester and help my sister with a rather difficult problem. I don't have the time for your prevarications."

"Is this because I…"

"Pushed me away for six weeks and pretended everything was normal. Kissing you… being with you… was everything I wanted. From your reactions, I believed it was what you wanted too."

"It is." More than even David could have admitted to himself.

Humphrey shrugged his shoulders. "It's terribly convenient of you to realise this just as I have to dedicate my time to something that isn't you."

David gritted his teeth. "Do you really see me as so selfish?"

"I'm not going to answer that. You hurt me, David. I have to go before my father makes another bad decision."

David stepped backwards, stunned at the comment. "After everything your father did, you still rush to help him?"

"After everything I've done for you, you still don't see it, do you?"

"I don't understand." David couldn't find a logical connection between how Humphrey's father treated him and how Humphrey saw himself in his role with David's projects.

Humphrey shook his head. "Never mind. I'm going to help my sister Elspeth. She's always been loyal to me."

"Oh." Could it be that simple? Complex problems often had simple solutions and suddenly David realised he'd taken

Humphrey's loyalty and continually dismissed it for years. Humphrey needed loyalty in return.

"I'm coming to support you. It's taken me too long to admit the depth of my feelings for you, and if it takes me as long again to demonstrate them to you, then it's only fair."

"Don't treat me like an account book." Humphrey stood up, clutching the letter from his sister, and marched out of the overseer's tent. His shoulder brushed against David, leaving steam behind like cold water thrown on a hot pan, as he squeezed past in the small space.

CHAPTER TEN

Humphrey didn't have to rush off to help his sister. His presence wasn't going to change Father's mind. But after six weeks of watching David pretend nothing had changed between them, he had to do something. Resentment filled his chest, and it mixed with hope and frustration. Even after everything, David still refused to trust that Humphrey was loyal and wouldn't leave him. The moment he'd opened his mouth and told David he was leaving, he realised the threat wasn't the answer either. He shouldn't need to hurt David to get him to see him. The situation was forlorn. At what point did Humphrey walk away with the sad knowledge that David would never care as much as he did? And then hope fluttered and grew. David was willing to leave his work behind for Humphrey, to be with him, to put him first. If only Humphrey could trust the change in David's priorities. He marched down to the collier and negotiated with the captain who was pleased to have some paying custom for the return trip. Ironic really, given that the Canal project had already paid for the round trip to get the supplies they needed on time. Shipping iron for the lock mechanisms was an expensive business.

Hours later, Humphrey sat in his small cabin alone. The air pressed on him. What on earth had he done? He shuffled papers pointlessly; he could have, should have simply written a letter to his sister and stayed with David on the project. But he'd wanted space from endlessly wanting David and getting nothing in return.

The door swung open and hit the wall with a clunk.

"Humphrey."

"Yes?"

David stood in the doorway, his shoulders filling the space. "I have a confession."

"Fine." Humphrey couldn't find the energy for more of this. He'd done everything in his power to move their relationship forward and David had continually pushed back at him. It wasn't worth it. Humphrey had finally realised he couldn't maintain this one-sided life. He poured energy in and it disappeared into a sink-hole, an exercise in futility.

"Kissing you scared me."

"We were drunk. It doesn't have to mean anything."

David growled and walked towards him, each step stalking him. "It matters. You matter. That's why I spent so long trying to pretend it didn't."

"Six weeks or ten years?"

"Both. Ten years ago, you were so young, a fresh faced

youth with all the world ahead of you. You didn't need an affair with a jaded older man."

"Older? You are only eight years older than me."

David waved his hands, an out of character movement. "Yes. When we met, when you first worked as an apprentice on one of my projects, every one of those years mattered. You were eighteen. I was twenty-six and your boss."

"And you've been using that as an excuse ever since." Humphrey was tired of this discussion, of being seen as less than David, and too young to make his own choices.

"I know." David nodded, his expression softly serious. "You became my equal a long time ago. In many ways, you became my better, but if we are simply talking about power; we are business partners now. Equals under law. All my excuses for not kissing you back then aren't valid anymore."

Humphrey nearly fell out of his chair in shock and covered it up by standing awkwardly. "You thought about kissing me back then?" He'd assumed his lust had always been one sided.

David shook his head, a rueful twist to his smile. "You have no idea, do you? Everyone was charmed by you from the beginning. They are still charmed by you. Everywhere you go, the men are glad they didn't have their wives or daughters on site, and the few men who are our way inclined are obviously taken by you too."

"I only had eyes for you." Humphrey held his breath.

"You hid it extremely well. It's not an excuse, of course. I'm the one who kissed you, who touched you, then ignored you. I could point to my own issues, but the truth of the matter, the real crux of it, is that kissing you scared me. I realised I couldn't lose you; you matter too much to me."

Humphrey let out the breath in a hot rush. "Because of the business and the work."

"That's been my excuse, yes. It's only partly true. You matter to me on a deeply personal level. You complement my skills with your skills. I could never have achieved any of this without you, and that scared me. It still scares me because if you leave, I won't be able to work without you. I didn't want to risk everything I've worked to create."

Humphrey yearned to believe him. He imagined a table full of his favourite food, all laid out for him, ready to be enjoyed, and yet, he still knew that David controlled the door. At any point, he could close the door and take away everything Humphrey wanted before he'd had a taste.

"I've been completely selfish with regards to your feelings. So caught up in my own drive, my own worries, that I didn't think about you at all. I'm sorry. I want to change and be there for you."

Humphrey sighed. "I don't want you to change, David. I just want you to see me. I want to be noticed."

"I don't..."

"I know you don't understand. That's the issue. I want you to notice that I've always been here for you. I can't be in your life without you seeing me anymore."

David stepped closer, and gently traced his fingers over Humphrey's jaw. "Let me finish. I do see you. For a long time, I convinced myself I didn't want to notice your loyalty, your brilliance, and your wonderful smile. That you gave those freely to everyone so I wasn't special to you. I was wrong. I was scared because I knew that when I did notice, I'd fall to my knees before you, hold you tight and never want to let go. If you think that I'm driven in my need to create engineering projects that will change the world, wait until you feel the force of my love for you."

"You love me?" Humphrey's heart pounded.

"I have for years."

"I don't believe you."

"I didn't want to believe it either. I pushed the feeling away, hid it in a cupboard where I didn't have to deal with it. It took one drunken night to open the cupboard door and let some of those feelings out. Of course, my instinct was to shove them back in there and try to ignore them. I couldn't take the risk that you might leave me if I told you how I really felt. I want to love you openly."

Humphrey raised one eyebrow; one day he'd tell David about his own door analogy. Not just yet. He wanted to hear everything David had to say.

"Obviously, not as openly as I'd like. I'm not going to sacrifice your safety, or my own, just to tell the world how incredible you are."

"David. Relax. I understand the balance we must undertake. And thank you."

"I want to stop fighting myself. I love you, Humphrey. I didn't want to admit that you've always been there for me. I've made so many mistakes and wasted so much time trying to find someone else, someone less important to me, so I didn't have to face the way I feel about you."

Humphrey swallowed. "I want to believe you."

David leaned in close and brushed his lips across

Humphrey's mouth. "Please believe me. I love you. Whole-heartedly and with everything I have. I know I'll have to get better at showing you my truth."

Humphrey smiled. "Relax David. I've worked with you for years. It often takes you a lot of time to analyse a situation and come to a decision, but once it's made, you'll stick with it."

David blinked a few times slowly. "You are so right. I'd decided, a long time ago, that you weren't for me. Too young, too vibrant, too many excuses. And I couldn't let myself change my decision, even when the weight of new data forced me to reanalyse."

"Spoken like a true engineer." Humphrey laughed, and a ball of tension released from his shoulders.

"Damn, I love you." David shook his head and laughed too. "Why did I fight against this for so long?"

Humphrey couldn't resist. "Obviously, you needed a worthy adversary."

"I don't want to fight myself anymore."

Laughter caught in his chest and he let it spill out, loud and sure. "Trust you to frame this so egotistically. How about we go forward as equal partners, as lovers? I would promise no more arguing, but I get the impression that you rather enjoy my brand of banter."

"I do. Very much." David pulled Humphrey into a huge hug. "Tonight, when we are alone in our room with no prying eyes to see, I will show you exactly how much I love and adore you."

Humphrey kissed David firmly on the mouth and he

tasted like forever. "Tonight, and every night from now on. I don't wish to be parted from you again."

"I see no reason why we should ever be apart from this day forth. You've demonstrated that you will be there for me and my work, and I will honour your commitment with my own. I love you, you illogical, charming, wonderful man."

I hope you enjoyed reading LOVE WASN'T BUILT IN A DAY. Sign up to my newsletter at reneedahlia.com to discover more mm romances.

If you want more historical mm romance, why not try HIS LORD'S SOLDIER?

Two best friends torn apart by war. Could the re-enactment of four Christmas dinners create a love worth fighting for?

Lord Rafe Stanmore didn't just lose his leg in the war; he lost his charming outlook and all his athletic prowess. His best friend, James St. George, brought him through the worst times with his cheerful letters. Rafe can't bear to face James now he's so altered, but to placate his sister he agrees to a quick visit. His secret longing for James and the nightly re-lived trauma of the war should be able to stay hidden for a few days.

During the war, James tried to declare his love for Rafe with careful words and extravagant gifts, and never had any indication of his affection being reciprocated. How could gorgeous, athletic, and aristocratic Rafe be interested in polio scarred James? But when Rafe arrives at the farm unexpectedly, James can't resist giving him all the Christmases he missed. It's his last chance to show Rafe exactly how he feels.

Four Christmases to reveal a passion that can't be denied. One last chance to admit the love they've been hiding all along.

ACKNOWLEDGMENTS

I acknowledge the Wangal people of the Eora Nation, who are the traditional custodians of the land on which this book was written. I pay my respects to the Elders past and present.

Thank you Ebony for creating the anthology that this novella was originally published in and for inventing the Soho Club.

AUTHOR NOTES

This novella is essentially Thomas Telford fan fiction. Telford was arguably England's greatest civil engineer; and many of the most beautiful bridges in England were designed by him. Of note are the Menai Bridge, the Pontcysyllte Aqueduct, the Caledonian Canal system, the Holyhead Road, the Conwy Bridge, and the Waterloo Bridge. David Mattson is based on Telford and is named after Matthew Davidson, Telford's close friend and business partner. The quoted letter in the first chapter is real, although I changed out Telford's name and replaced it with the fictional poet Sutherland. The poet Robert Southey wrote it in his diary after accompanying Telford for a six week tour of the Highland projects in 1819. During those six weeks, Telford and Southey were "never out of each other's company, often sharing great discomforts and the same bedroom in many indifferent and primitive Highland inns," according to LTC Rolt's biography of Thomas Telford. There is such raw emotion in Southey's quote that I couldn't resist using it.

The Caledonian Canal was a commercial failure that was expected to take seven years to complete, but took twelve years, and went £436,000 over budget, with loans from the government beginning in 1808 and continuing under a mechanism that was later formalised in 1817 as the Public Works Loan Board, as well as private investment in the scheme. It wasn't completed until 1822 and cost a total of £910,000 (2020 £118,238,600).

Nearly half of the 1811 loan "commissioners" were evangelical Christians and had been appointed by fellow evangelist Spencer Perceval.

Whether Telford and PM Spencer Perceval had any interaction in real life is unknown, although possible. As this book is fiction and only loosely based on Telford, I've stretched this possibility into fictional reality.

ALL BOOKS BY RENÉE DAHLIA

Thanks for reading LOVE WASN'T BUILT IN A DAY. I hope you enjoyed it.

Reviews can help readers find books, and I am grateful for all honest reviews. Thank you for taking the time to let others know what you've read, and what you thought.

If you write a review for LOVE WASN'T BUILT IN A DAY and email me with the link, I will send you a free copy of any of my other books of your choice. My email is renee@reneedahlia.com.

If you'd like to know more about me, my books, or to connect with me online, you can visit my webpage

www.reneedahlia.com

and if you sign up to my newsletter, you can grab a free book.

Twitter https://twitter.com/dekabat
Facebook https://www.facebook.com/
reneedahliawriter/
Instagram https://www.instagram.com/
reneedahlia_author/
Patreon https://www.patreon.com/reneedahlia
BookBub https://www.bookbub.com/authors/
renee-dahlia

Historical Series: Desiring the Dexingtons

1. Love Wasn't Built in a Day (mm)
2. The Secret Life of Spinsters (ff)
3. The Widow's Modiste (ff)

Historical Series: Great War

1. Her Lady's Melody (ff)
2. Her Lady's Fortune (ff)
3. Her Lady's Honor (ff)
4. His Lord's Soldier (mm)

Historical Series: Bluestockings

Prequel: The Shipwrecked Earl's Bride (fm with bisexual hero)
1. To Charm a Bluestocking (fm with bisexual hero)
2. In Pursuit of a Bluestocking (fm)
3. The Heart of a Bluestocking (fm)

Contemporary Series: Gamble Racing

1. Driven to Distraction (mm)
2. Driven by Passion (mm)
3. Driven by Ambition (mm)
4. Driven to Protect (mm)

Contemporary Series: Seraph's Burlesque Club

1. Show Up (ff with bisexual heroine)
2. Show Off (ff with bisexual heroines)
3. Show Queen (ff)
4. Show Time (mm)
5. Show Dance (mm)

Contemporary Series: Kapow!

1. Out of Her League (fm with bisexual characters)
2. His Buxom Beauty (fm)
3. Craving His Spotlight (mm)
4. Her Pregnant Rival (ff)

Contemporary Series: Farrellton Foster Family

1. Betrayed (fm)
2. Forbidden (fm with bisexual characters)
3. Liability (ff)

Contemporary Series: Margaret River TV: Boxed Set

- Homage (fm with bisexual heroine)
- Uplift (ff with bisexual heroines)

Contemporary Series: Merindah Park

1. Merindah Park (fm)
2. Making Her Mark (fm with bisexual heroine)
3. Two Hearts Healing (fm)
4. Racetrack Royalty (fm)

Contemporary Series: Rainbow Cove

1. His Christmas Pearl (fm)
2. His Christmas Pride (mm)